BEAST BUSINESS

HIDDEN LEGACY

BOOK 7

ILONA ANDREWS

ACKNOWLEDGMENTS

The authors would like to thank the following people for their help, time, and patience:

Rossana Sasso for her editorial guidance;

Stephanie Chin for the copyedit and Lindsi Root for the proofread;

Helena Elias for the incredible cover;

Natanya Wheeler for the ebook formatting and Sarah for the text design;

Megan McElroy, OR Nurse First Assist, and loyal member of the BDH and Fulvia Franchini for their medical expertise - all errors of fact are our own;

Harriet Chow, Kerris Humphreys, Louise McCoy Vickers, Francesca Virgili for beta reading the manuscript

INTRODUCTION

If you are new to the Hidden Legacy or if you are returning after a long absence, the short section below might refresh your memory or catch you up to speed.

The Lore

In 1863, in a world much like our own, European scientists tried to cure the flu and discovered the Osiris serum instead, a concoction which brought out one's magic talents. These talents were many and varied. Some people gained the ability to command animals, some learned to sense water from miles away, and others suddenly realized they could kill their enemies by throwing lightning from their fingertips.

The serum spread through the planet. It was given to soldiers in hopes of making military forces more deadly. It was obtained by members of the fading aristocracy, desperate to hold on to power. It was bought by the rich, who desired to get richer. The magic users were evaluated and sorted into ranks starting with Minors, who had bare whispers of magic at their disposal, all the way to Primes, mages of incredible power.

Eventually the world realized the consequences of awakening godlike powers in ordinary people. The serum was locked away, but it was too late. The magic talents passed on from parents to their children had changed the course of human history forever. The future of entire nations shifted in the span of a few short decades. Those who previously married for status, money, and power now married for magic, because strong magic would give them everything.

Now, a century and a half later, families with strong hereditary magic have evolved into dynasties. These families—Houses, as they call themselves—own corporations, control their own territories within the cities, and influence politics. They employ private armies, they feud with each other, and their disputes are deadly. It is a world where the more magic you have, the more prominent and successful you are. Some magic talents are destructive. Some are subtle. Some Houses are powerful and wealthy. Others are much less so. But no magic user should be taken lightly.

Magic Ranks and Types

There are five magic ranks, from weakest to strongest: Minor – Average – Notable – Significant – Prime.

There are three main categories of magic: elemental, mental, and arcane.

Elemental mages control air, water, fire, and earth. They part seas, extract minerals, and alter the weather.

Mental mages possess the powers of the mind. They are deadly telekinetics, crafters of incredible weapons, and human lie detectors.

Arcane mages include those who do not fit into either of these categories. They are metamorphosis mages (shifters), summoners who pluck strange creatures from a magical dimension, and those who can enhance their bodies.

Houses

A House is a magic family that produces at least three Primes (highest rated magic users) in two generations. They are the elite of magical society.

This story is about three Houses bound together by a friendship pact:

House Montgomery, led by Augustine Montgomery, a Prime famous for his illusion magic, who controls Montgomery International Investigations (MII), the largest and most powerful PI firm in the Southwest;

House Baylor, a family whose talents are strange and varied and who runs Baylor Investigations, a much smaller and more boutique PI firm that specializes in complex cases requiring unusual care. One of their members is Arabella Baylor, the youngest of the Baylor siblings;

And **House Harrison**, led by Diana Harrison, a family whose power lies in bonding with animals, giving them unique perspectives and distancing them from other humans. Despite that distance, Diana Harrison views the Baylors as family and House Montgomery as steadfast allies.

Cast of Characters

People marked by * are mentioned but they do not appear in the story.

The Montgomerys:

Augustine Montgomery – Prime, head of House Montgomery and the CEO of Montgomery International Investigations (MII,) one of the larger PI firms in the country. Illusion mage.

*Verena Montgomery – Augustine's younger sister, friends with Arabella Baylor. Illusion mage.

The Baylors:

Arabella Baylor – Prime, Magic sealed, the youngest member of House Baylor. Despite her age, Arabella has a lot of investigative experience, having worked for her family business since she was a teenager.

*Bern Baylor – Arabella's older cousin, who was adopted into the family.

*Catalina Baylor – Arabella's older sister and the Head of House Baylor

*Nevada Rogan (Baylor) – Arabella's oldest sister who married Connor Rogan, Augustine's best friend, and joined his House.

The Harrisons:

Diana Harrison – Prime, head of House Harrison. Animal mage.

*Cornelius Harrison – Diana's youngest brother and a private investigator who works for Baylor Investigations. His wife, Nari, was murdered, and the Baylors helped him find the culprit and exact his revenge, after which he joined their firm.

Matilda Harrison – Cornelius' nine-year-old daughter.

*Blake Harrison – Diana's younger brother.

BEAST BUSINESS

[1]

"As you know, Maria, the current state of the economy requires our company to develop agility in an effort to meet the rapidly changing realities of the marketplace."

The HR manager smiled, her hand resting on a black folder with *FINERGY* etched in gold on it. She was in her forties. Her makeup had been applied with technical precision. Her acrylic nails, translucent pink and of a professionally acceptable length, bore small white Easter eggs as a nod to the holiday season. A rose quartz necklace dripped from her neck, each bead polished, matching the nails and the nearly transparent pink frames of her eyeglasses.

She seemed plastic, having been poured into a corporate mold, allowed to harden, extracted, polished, and then placed in the conference room, with her rigid smile and by-the-book hair. A kind of generic mass-produced middle manager.

The two men sitting on either side of her had come from the same factory and wore identical expressions of dutiful concern for the office drone they were about to cut loose. A united front, in case there were issues.

"In light of these developments, we've had to make some difficult decisions."

The corporate *we*. Fun thing about polished plastic—it tended to be slick. Nothing stuck to it, responsibility included.

"We've decided to go in a different direction, Maria."

First name basis, designed to provide the illusion of a caring professional relationship. *We are all family here. Surely you understand. Nothing personal, Maria.*

"You've been an asset to our team; however, we must reduce our overhead obligations."

You are not a person, Maria. This was badly handled. Painfully drawn out, full of empty platitudes. Just abysmal.

"We've chosen to let you go."

Finally.

"Try not to see this as a setback, but rather a new opportunity to learn lessons and apply them in your future endeavors."

No, not just badly handled. Gloriously badly handled, as if they had made it a point to check every box of what not to do when firing an employee. *Now tell me you will walk me to the door...*

"Cory will walk you to the door."

And we have a home run.

"Good luck, Maria. We are rooting for you."

The temptation to golf clap was almost too much, but it would've been irresponsible under the circumstances. Arrangements like these came with certain expectations, and they had to be honored.

The box they offered was too large for the meager possessions living on the desk. Sweeping them into the box under Cory's watchful gaze took mere seconds. An elevator ride followed, the mirror inside offering a reflection of Cory, stone-faced in a Brooks Brothers suit, looming over a woman in her thirties, olive-skinned, dark hair cut into a bob, a blouse from

Torrid a size too large, the consequence of stress-induced weight loss. Quite the contrast.

The trek across a wide lobby was next, complete with pitying glances from former co-workers, at once sympathetic and wary, as if instead of a defeated woman in business attire they had spied a leper in filthy rags and worried the disease might spread.

The glass doors of Callas Tower swung open, offering freedom and overcast daylight. Cory walked out and planted himself in front of the door, ready to put his life on the line to protect the firm's secrets in case the ex-employee decided to assault the building.

Too little, too late.

It was time for a dejected walk down the street and out of sight.

The city was going about its business, oblivious to the small tragedies of firings in the name of corporate agility. Thick grey clouds clogged the sky, promising prompt rain, common to Houston in April.

A gunmetal-grey BMW SUV slid closer to the curb, its electric motor nearly silent, and the rear passenger window slid down, revealing a woman's face. She was beautiful in a quiet way. Light brown eyes, flecked with gold and framed by naturally long eyelashes. A lovely face. Chestnut hair, braided in a kind of updo that would have been too soft and romantic for the HR trio in the conference room.

Diana Harrison, Prime and the head of House Harrison. She'd cut her hair and changed her hair color. It suited her better. Her usual icy blonde always felt soulless somehow. Too cold.

Diana tilted her head. "May I offer you a ride?"

"Do we know each other?"

She smiled without parting her lips. "Not closely, but it's about to rain and your office is at least twenty minutes away."

Oh. She knew. How?

There was no point in playing coy. "In that case, thank you. I'll join you."

A driver emerged, took the box, and opened the back door on the other side. Getting in took only a moment. A large red Doberman sat in the front passenger seat, strapped in by some strange seatbelt contraption, her gaze alert and watchful.

The dog could've picked up the scent and alerted, but not through a closed window. How had Diana known?

The car slid back into traffic.

Letting go was like a light, imaginary stretch. A brief effort, followed by a slight lessening of the load.

Gone was the olive skin, the short dark bob, the blouse, and the utilitarian black slacks. He was tall again, his regular persona firmly in place, familiar like an old glove. His true self still remained hidden, yet the new illusion was a tweak rather than an entirely new disguise. Like taking off a sweater but keeping the T-shirt on.

He stretched for real this time, working a kink out of his shoulders. The hunched posture had taken a bit of a toll.

He hadn't needed to slouch, strictly speaking, but he always found that his illusions flowed better when he allowed himself to fully submerge into his assumed identity. After that barrage, most people in Maria's place would have either stormed out defiantly or braced themselves, as if expecting to be punched. Storming out wouldn't have achieved his goals.

Diana watched him with genuine fascination. He'd seen that reaction so many times that he should've been used to it by now, but coming from her it felt refreshing.

"A moment?"

Diana nodded.

He pulled his cell phone out of his Zegna suit and selected his second-in-command from the contact list.

Zachary answered instantly. "Here."

"Dump FINERGY."

"Understood."

He ended the call, tossed one long leg over the other, and smiled.

"I believe I will dump FINERGY as well," Diana said.

"Professionally, no comment. Personally, off the record, I highly recommend it. They are engaged in cybersecurity fraud. The latest crop of drones they brought to the market and sold to multiple law enforcement agencies has severe software issues. Allegedly."

"How severe?"

"A child with a LeapFrog tablet could hack one. They just fired the specialist who brought the problem to their attention two months ago."

"You assumed her identity?"

He nodded. The scale of the fraud was massive enough that the real Maria's safety was a concern. He'd spent the last week dutifully going to the office in her place. Normally, he would've sent one of his subordinates, but his House's investment in FINERGY was considerable, and he had wanted to assess the state of things for himself.

Diana tapped her phone.

Tomorrow one of the biggest law firms in Houston would file the *qui tam* lawsuit against FINERGY, alleging violations of the False Claims Act, and Maria would become one of the most famous whistleblowers on record. If the government chose to join the suit, she would be entitled to about twenty percent of recovered damages. Considering the extent of FINERGY's transgressions, she wouldn't have to worry about finding a new job for some time.

Diana finished and put her phone down. "Now I'm in your debt, Prime Montgomery."

"Not at all. We never spoke of this." He slid his glasses a little higher on his nose. "Please, call me Augustine. Now then, what can Montogomery International Investigations do for House Harrison?"

Diana hesitated. It was very brief, but he'd been trained to observe people carefully, noting minute changes in expression.

"I want to hire you."

"Me specifically or MII in general?"

"Both."

Intriguing. "In what capacity?"

Another slight hesitation. There was something deceptively delicate about Diana. She was a small woman, short and petite. The contours of her face were soft, her features classically attractive: large, beautiful eyes, a small, slightly upturned nose, a full mouth with a bare hint of pink lipstick. She looked as if she were teetering on the edge, torn between wanting to keep her secret and asking for help. She could've played a princess in a medieval drama, the kind who had suffered an injustice and needed a strong ally. The kind who would inspire the audience to root for her.

It was a front. Augustine was absolutely sure of it. If he became an enemy, Diana Harrison would attempt to kill him without a moment's hesitation. She was trying to entice him to help her and make her request a priority, and she was very subtle about it.

Common wisdom held that animal mages didn't understand human emotions. They formed bonds with animals through the power of their magic, and that process fundamentally altered their thinking, stunting their emotional development and making their interactions with other people difficult. Interacting with Cornelius, Diana's brother, had convinced Augustine that there were exceptions to that rule. Apparently, Diana was cut from the same cloth.

He knew a great deal about her, and at the same time very little. They'd met on three occasions prior to today, and his longest interaction with Diana had happened when they signed the pact of friendship between their two Houses. The alliance was initiated by Cornelius, who had become convinced that having powerful connections was the best way to keep his daughter safe. As the head of her House, Diana was the only one with the authority to sign off on it, so they had met to negotiate.

Entering a pact of friendship was a no-brainer. While most Houses viewed animal mages as having limited power with few practical applications, to an illusion House there was no greater threat. He'd been delighted to neutralize it. His people had done a deep dive into House Harrison and found nothing of concern. On all three occasions he'd interacted with Diana, her demeanor was neutral, pleasant, and opaque. She had negotiated in good faith. This manipulation was delightfully new.

"Whether or not we come to an agreement, anything and everything you tell me is confidential," he said.

"Something has been stolen from us," she said.

"And you need me to find the culprit and recover it?"

Diana nodded.

"Why MII? Pardon me for stating the obvious, but you have access to House Baylor through your brother."

Cornelius worked with the Baylors as a private investigator. The two families connected after the Baylors helped him discover who murdered his wife.

"The Baylors specialize in outside-the-box investigations," Augustine continued. "Considering how close your families are, they would give your problem first priority."

"The Baylors can't be involved in this matter," she said.

Curiouser and curiouser.

His own relationship with House Baylor was complicated. At one point, before the Baylors became a House and had just been a small PI agency, he owned the mortgage on their business. Prior to his death, his father had made a habit of offering financing to small PI firms who needed an influx of cash, a practice Augustine had since ended. The Baylors had been one of those mortgaged subcontractors, and he paid them no attention until a difficult client forced him to reach for a creative solution. In retrospect, it had been a negligent decision at best and morally bankrupt one at worst, and it temporarily put his House and the Baylor family into adversarial positions.

Later, House Montgomery and House Baylor came to regard each other as allies, especially once Connor Rogan, the closest person he had to a friend, married Nevada Baylor. The Baylors and he signed an alliance pact, an agreement that obligated them to respond if either House was threatened. So far, they had kept their word, and as long as he kept his, their loyalty and support were assured.

He always thought that the Harrisons and Baylors had an even deeper connection. The Baylors thought of Cornelius and his daughter, Matilda, as their family, but now Diana was implying that they couldn't be trusted.

Either way, he had to draw the line now. As much as he valued the Harrisons, his House's relationship with the Rogans and the Baylors mattered more. It wasn't an alliance he was willing to endanger.

"Are the Baylors suspects?"

"No. They had nothing to do with this."

"And they don't know anything about it?"

Diana shook her head.

He saw it now. She baited the hook, offering him just enough information to ignite his curiosity, and waited for him to bite. Diana Harrison, a patient and careful fisherwoman.

In strict terms, their friendship pact was a non-aggression alliance, meaning that both Houses agreed to refrain from acting against each other. Mutual favors were not included but were customary in such arrangements. The disparity in their wealth, connections, and resources was significant, and yet House Harrison had asked for his help only once, when they needed him to pick up Matilda and secure her safety until Diana came to retrieve her.

Very well. Why not? He could play a knight in shining armor, if the compensation was significant enough and Diana offered payment in the right kind of currency. Most investigative work was profitable and boring. This promised to be interesting. He liked knowing secrets, and any secret hidden from the Baylors was worth knowing.

"Shall we discuss the details in my office?" he asked.

She offered him a beautiful smile.

Augustine's office lay on the seventeenth floor. He'd chosen that location precisely because it satisfied his requirements for being high up but lacked the ostentatious statement of a top-floor office. During his tenure as the CEO of MII, his father had occupied the penthouse business suite. When Augustine officially took the reins of MII, he resolved to never enter it again, and he hadn't set foot there in years.

The elevator doors whispered open, and he invited Diana forward with a sweep of his hand. They walked across the spotless dark blue floor through his kingdom of tall white walls and cobalt-tinted light streaming through the sheath of blue windows that wrapped around the building.

He watched Diana's expression covertly. Her face was relaxed and pleasant, her eyes calm. Prime Harrison moved with smooth grace, almost gliding across the floor, and the Doberman at her side matched her stride. The dog's natural ears were down, her mouth half-open in a canine smile. He had seen enough Dobermans in his line of work. They were cautious dogs, alert and restrained in a new environment. This one was doing a fine impression of a golden retriever. There was an odd synergy between the woman and the dog—both sleek, assured, and pretending to be harmless.

They reached his office, where Lina sat at a pristine desk, presenting the last line of defense to the visitors. The desk was crafted from polished metal, with a single white orchid growing from a simple pot. His secretary chose to match the orchid today. A white dress hugged her body, perfectly tailored and form-fitting, yet elegant. Her deep emerald hair, wrapped in a trendy twist, shimmered with peridot highlights. Her eyebrows were black and shaped with laser precision, and she had selected green and black eye shadow to accent her eyes and mauve to tint her lips. As always, the effect was stunning.

Unfortunately, his newest intern had referred to that precise shade of mauve as "hot dog lips," and now he could not divorce himself from it. Mentoring the youngest Baylor child came with its own annoyances.

He nodded to Lina and led his visitor to the right, where a translucent wall of frosted glass hid his office space. A nearly seamless door swung open, and Augustine paused on the side, letting Diana enter. She walked in and sat in a chair, smoothing the skirt of her elegant grey business suit with a practiced gesture. The Doberman dropped on the floor to her right. Not a concern in the world.

Augustine sat behind his desk. His office was located in the corner where two walls of blue glass met at an angle, and from his vantage point, he had a wide view of Downtown Houston. Unlike most people, he loved heights.

Diana glanced at a sign on the right wall, a quote without attribution. *Trust Not Too Much in Appearances.*

"Virgil," she said.

It appeared that House Harrison believed in a classical education. "It's a reminder," he said.

"To you or to your visitors?"

"To me. We do our best to convince our visitors that we are trustworthy."

"Is that why you chose a modern aesthetic for the building?"

He nodded. "Most people who want to hire an illusion mage come to us unsure what they might find. Consciously or subconsciously, they expect to be deceived. Our business requires trust, so we keep the interior simple, almost austere. Long unbroken walls, concrete floors, and transparent glass leave little room for illusions. People find it reassuring."

"I see."

She wasn't giving him very much to work with.

"Are you truly trustworthy, Prime Montgomery?"

Augustine leaned back in his chair. "That depends on your definition of trust. Will I keep everything you tell me confidential, and will I do everything in my ability to help you if we reach an agreement? Yes."

"In that case, would you mind answering a question before we begin?"

His guess was proving accurate. Nothing about this visit would be boring. "That depends on the question."

Diana gave him a small smile, but her eyes remained watchful.

"I know that Arabella Baylor visits this office twice a week, and she hasn't told her mother or her sister, Catalina, about it."

Diana's gaze turned direct and unblinking. She likely felt protective toward the Baylors. He wasn't obligated to explain, but good business relationships relied on trust. And it was a reasonable question. Catalina, Arabella's sister, was the Head of the House. Anything hidden from the Head of the House usually wasn't good.

Augustine reached into his desk, took out a folder, and offered it to her.

Diana glanced at the contents. "Internship agreement signed

by Nevada Rogan? Arabella's oldest sister gave her permission for this?"

"My sister graduated from Donovan High." Normally he had a knee-jerk reaction to avoid speaking about his family, but for some reason it didn't trigger in her presence.

Diana's eyebrows rose. "Donovan? Not Heritage?"

Of the two high schools catering to the magically gifted, Heritage was far more prestigious. If you were a scion of a House, you went to Heritage, while Donovan took the rest.

"Yes. She attended under an assumed name."

And an assumed persona. If Verena's former classmates ever met her off school grounds, they wouldn't recognize her. Except for Arabella, none of them had any idea what his sister truly looked like.

"The principal and the senior staff were aware of who she was," he continued. "My sister wanted it that way, and I acquiesced."

"Arabella also attended Donovan," Diana said.

"Yes. They are friends."

The strangest friendship that sprouted from a bizarre crisis. It made sense. Both children had been held back a year, both were the oldest students in their graduating class at 19, and now both were doing the transitional post-graduation program designed to pad their college applications because neither qualified for the school of their choice without it.

The old him would have never expected his sister to be held back or struggle with her academics. He would've expected Verena to blaze to the Valedictorian spot and have her pick of schools the way Seraphina had.

A familiar cold vise squeezed his throat. Losing a sibling fundamentally altered his expectations for his remaining sister, brother, and the cousin he had taken in. He was less of a brother now and more of a parent, and he went from expecting traditional success and academic excellence to celebrating minute signs that they were slowly but steadily moving past the horror that almost destroyed their family.

Diana was waiting for him to elaborate.

"They're both enrolled in Path to College. It is a gap year program that offers AP courses, which makes students more attractive to college admission departments. Both Arabella and Verena are taking House Business Administration, which requires one hundred and sixty hours of an internship with a business owned by a House other than your family."

"You swapped," Diana said. "The Rogans took your sister, and you took Arabella."

He nodded. "It's an arrangement that works for both children. I know that Connor and Nevada will not put my sister in harm's way, and they understand that I will do the same for Arabella. Have I passed the trust test?"

"Yes."

"In that case, how may I help you?"

"What I am about to tell you is secret," Diana said. "And I would kill to keep it that way in the literal sense of that word."

"Understood."

"Are you familiar with Zeus?"

"The Greek god or your brother's tiger?"

"The tiger."

She took a slim tablet from her purse, flicked her fingers across it, and showed it to him. On the screen, a massive animal stretched, vaguely feline, a distant cousin of a tiger if tigers had blue fur splattered with darker and paler rosettes and a fringe of six-inch-long tentacles around their necks.

All the magic talents in the world fit into three broad categories: elemental, mental, and arcane. The elemental mages commanded the proverbial elements—fire, water, weather and so on. The mental mages displayed powers of the mind, like telekinesis, illusion, and truthseeking. Everything else, everything that was odd and unusual, fit into the category of arcane.

Of the arcane discipline, summoning was one of the least understood. Summoners reached into the arcane realm, a place of magic outside of normal reality, called forth monstrous creatures, and hurled these biological weapons at their opponents. Nobody knew exactly how any of it worked, and the summoners were not forthcoming with explanations.

Creatures brought over by weaker summoners vanished when their temporary masters lost focus. Monsters conjured by upper-level mages stayed in the world permanently, but most summoned creatures had short lifespans, even with the best of care. They withered, like repotted plants that failed to take root. Sometimes it took days, sometimes weeks, but eventually all arcane creatures perished. With the exception of the organisms that were planted into a human host.

Zeus had been plucked from an arcane realm by a summoner Prime, who used him to attack Nevada Baylor and Diana's brother, Cornelius. Somehow during that confrontation, Cornelius had tamed Zeus against all odds, severing the link between the creature and the summoner.

Augustine had looked into it after the incident. No animal mage on record had even been able to bond with a summoned beast. Cornelius was the only exception, and the bond between them somehow kept Zeus alive and thriving.

"We decided to call the species Tigrionex," Diana said.

Tigris, Latin for tiger, and *nex* meaning violent death. "Tiger of slaughter?"

"Yes." Diana slid her finger across the tablet. Another image appeared, still of Zeus. Wait, no. This blue tiger was slightly different. It looked a little smaller, and its blue fur had a slight purple tint.

Augustine glanced at Diana. "You obtained a second tiger?"

She nodded. "Cornelius and I had purchased her at great expense. She had been manifested by a Prime summoner during a feud with a rival House and critically injured in that fight. They agreed to sell her to us because she was dying."

The cost must've been astronomical.

"Her name is Celeste. I was able to form a pact with her."

"Not Hera?"

"No. We didn't want to jinx it."

House Harrison had access to two summoned beasts, and both of them had bonded to their tamers. Clearly, there was something special about that family.

"Zeus and Celeste were allowed to mate. Before you ask, it was voluntary on their part. We would never exercise our influence over our animals to force a breeding. It was a difficult pregnancy."

"What about cloning or surrogacy?" he asked.

"That would have meant taking the choice away from them."

So they would risk a massive investment for the sake of maintaining the animals' autonomy. Interesting.

"We almost lost the mother, but in the end a single cub was born."

Another swipe of her fingers, and a new image. A shockingly adorable blue cub, all fluff, big eyes, and oversized paws. He wasn't given to sentimentality, but even he had to admit that the cuteness was off the charts.

An arcane creature born in this world. He could think of several highly educated magic experts who would argue that this little beast couldn't exist and would happily die on that hill.

If anyone found out about this, the Harrisons would come under massive pressure. Some would want to study the cub, some would want to purchase it, and others would want to kill it to keep the Harrisons from rising in power. A House who could breed and command arcane beasts. Not summon them with an expiration date but keep them, permanently. The potential was staggering.

"What's the cub's name?" he asked.

"We call her Kitty."

Augustine blinked.

"It's a placeholder name. We were hoping that when Kitty grew a little, Matilda would form a pact with her. My niece is very talented, and she sounds mature, but she is still a nine-year-old child. She makes reckless decisions. Cornelius and I will do everything in our power to protect her, but we cannot be everywhere at once."

And Kitty would grow up to be a formidable protector.

"These animals are different. They are smarter, more aware, and the bond with them is deeper," Diana said. "Every species is different when it comes to forming a connection. Tigers are solitary and self-sufficient. They have to be coaxed. Lions are clingy and social. They reach out. The tigrionex are like us, Augustine, inquisitive and social. They are curious about humans. They seem to like us and seek the bond, and they are persistent about it."

"Why do you think that is?"

"We don't know. But rebuffing an animal that seeks to bond that intensely is difficult. It feels unnatural. Especially when you are Matilda's age."

From the way she made it sound, if the child and the cub came in contact, the bond process would happen almost involuntarily.

Diana shifted in her chair, sliding one leg over the other. It wasn't a calculated movement, but he had to make a conscious effort not to linger on the lines of her body. The last time they'd met, it had been like that, too. He'd dismissed it as a passing attraction then, but it was worse now, with her in his client chair.

"Because of the difficult pregnancy, we decided to wait to introduce Matilda and the cub. We want to make sure Kitty survives. If Matilda bonds with her and the cub dies, the trauma to my niece would be catastrophic. That's why the Baylors can't be involved in this matter. Matilda spends most of her time at the Baylor compound. In the two months since they bought that estate, Matilda made friends with every mouse and bird on their property. She spies on the Baylors constantly. Nothing happens in that house that my niece doesn't know about."

"Can she hear through mouse ears?" he asked.

Diana looked at him for a second. "Vikilinta recording devices are one inch long, have the width of pencil graphite, and weigh nineteen grams. They're voice-activated and can record up to four hundred hours of audio. A healthy adult mouse weighs between forty and forty-five grams, can carry twice her body weight, and can be convinced to wear a harness."

And now he felt like a fool. What in the world was he thinking? The child was a budding Prime, not a mythical Beastmaster. Something about the connection between tech and animals always short-circuited his brain.

"Of course. However, I can't imagine the Baylors would look favorably on that kind of security breach."

"I've stressed the need for privacy to her multiple times," Diana said. "I do not believe her obsessive recording is malicious."

"Then why is she doing it?"

Diana sighed. Her face took on a slightly worn expression. "It is my understanding that a child subjected to early trauma, such as losing a mother in a horrific way, often seeks to establish control over her environment."

"Matilda is afraid that she will miss something vital and the people she cares about will die."

"Yes. You see now why we'd hidden the cub."

He understood perfectly.

"Matilda keeps the information she overhears confidential, unless something alarms her."

Ah. That's how Diana found out about Arabella's internship. Matilda must've discovered it and shared it with her aunt.

Diana studied him for another moment and turned the tablet toward him. On it, Kitty took shaky steps on stubby legs. She stumbled over to her frightening mother and batted at the otherworldly beast with her small paw. Celeste lowered her head. The cub tried to pounce, fell, and let out a frustrated noise, a tiny baby growl.

"You said something was stolen from you. They took the cub," he guessed.

"They did."

For a moment something vicious and cold shone through Diana's eyes. It seemed so incompatible with her usual demeanor, he wondered if he'd imagined it.

"When?"

"Yesterday."

"Have you received a ransom demand?"

"No."

"You need MII's help to find and recover Kitty," he said.

"Yes."

"You've gone to great lengths to keep Kitty's existence secret. Someone discovered it against all odds, infiltrated your security, and stole the cub. If this was a money grab, by now the kidnapper would've reached out. This tells me two things: the entity behind the theft wanted the cub for a specific purpose and the culprit is likely another House."

She nodded. "Yes."

They both knew what was left unsaid: a conflict like that meant House warfare. When Houses clashed, they paid the price not just in money, but in lives, and that cost could be staggering. Diana's face told him she understood all of that.

"Do you have any suspects?"

"No."

"If you had to guess?"

"Any animal mage would kill to possess a tigrionex," she said. "People know we have Zeus. We've had multiple offers from many Houses who want to purchase him. We rejected all of them. One of the Houses attempted to break the bond between Zeus and Cornelius."

"What happened?"

"They are no longer a House."

To become a House, a family had to produce three Primes in two generations. To remain a House, it had to have at least one living Prime. The Harrissons had killed at least one rival animal Prime. Possibly more.

"Kitty is still nursing," Diana said. "She requires her mother's milk to survive. There is no substitute. No formula. Without Celeste's milk, she will fall sick very quickly. We cannot wait."

"A recovery like that will be costly in every sense of that word. Although our Houses are in a friendship pact, even with that discount, the fee would be significant. Do you wish to see an estimate?"

"No. Whatever it takes. We will pay it."

"Are you sure?" The Harrisons were a House, but their talents didn't have many lucrative applications. He would put their total net worth under forty million.

"Absolutely. This isn't property, Prime Montgomery. This is a life."

Diana brushed her fingers over the recording. Her eyes shone with green, a sign of her magic activating.

"We welcomed Kitty into this world, we assumed responsibility for her, and now she is scared and alone. Celeste knows that her daughter is gone. I can feel her grief even now, through our bond. She relies on me to bring her home. Whatever it takes. Kitty must nurse in the next 24 hours, or we may lose her and Celeste both."

She looked up at him, and he glimpsed desperation in her expression.

"Will you help me, Augustine?"

He looked into her green and brown eyes, and the words came out before he realized he had spoken. "Of course, I will."

[2]

The office smelled of a mahogany fragrance with notes of teakwood.

Not a cologne. Augustine wasn't wearing any.

Not a deodorant. She had caught a faint whiff of that in the elevator. He was wearing Secret Outlast. His hair smelled like a synthetic fragrance blended with notes of aloe, argan oil, and camellia. Herbal Essences Argan Oil Repair, a familiar profile, one of many from the scent catalog stored in her memory. She collected scents the way some people accumulated vinyl records or crystals. When she saw him on the street, he looked like a businesswoman. He must've selected her preferred products to better impersonate her.

So thorough.

Not cologne, not deodorant, not shampoo… Ah. There it was. A scented candle in a tasteful jar of matte black glass on a small table in the corner. The lid was on, otherwise she would have pinpointed it sooner.

Diana raised her head from the contract. "I wish to add a stipulation."

Augustine nodded, his stunning face a picture of businesslike politeness. He was inhumanly beautiful. A prince, with his blond hair perfectly styled to complement his flawless features, elegant, confident, barely short of absolute perfection. She saw it for exactly what it was—armor.

Why? What was hiding behind the façade? Curiosity scratched at her with its needle claws.

She had long ago come to terms with parallel streams of thought running through her head. Wrangling all of them to focus on only one thing required pressing danger, and right now she didn't feel like her life was threatened.

"I need to accompany you in this investigation."

"In what capacity?"

"A partner," she said. "An employer. Backup. It doesn't matter. I want to be there, every step of the way."

He studied her. "The level of danger will be high. There may be times I cannot guarantee your safety."

"I know. I suggest that we spell it out in the contract. In the event of injury, I will hold MII blameless."

He leaned forward slightly.

There was something in his green eyes. Something... She couldn't put her finger on it, but it felt familiar.

"Prime Harrison..."

"Diana," she corrected. "As you said yourself, we might be in danger and yelling 'Prime Harrison' takes a lot longer."

"Diana," he said.

She liked his voice. It was smooth and rich. She liked the way he spoke, too, cultured, methodical, unhurried. More armor. He had been forthcoming and honest so far, but there was a distance there, as if they were having this conversation through a piece of transparent glass.

"This is unwise," he warned.

"I know."

"Can you tell me why? Is this a matter of trust?"

The rage shivered in her, spiking her hunting instincts into overdrive. She struggled with it, hiding behind a serene smile. He wouldn't understand. Most humans didn't understand. Cornelius would and so would her other brother, but Cornelius was across the ocean, in Germany, following a case, and Blake... Blake had very little interest in House matters. They were human problems, and he had chosen to interact with that side of himself only when he had exhausted all other options.

"Do I have to explain?" she asked.

"I'm afraid so."

He had told her about his sister and Arabella. She had to meet him halfway. That was fair, and fair was important.

"They took the cub from us. They took her, and Celeste is grieving. She cannot hunt the thief, so I must hunt in her stead."

"Hunt?"

"Yes. I cannot delegate this. It must be me." There was so much more there, but this would do for now.

Augustine sighed. "Very well." His fingers flew over the keyboard.

She had an urge to cross the room and lick the candle.

Augustine tapped his laptop. Her phone chimed. She checked the new contract. Adequate.

"Would an electronic signature suffice?"

"Of course."

She signed. He countersigned and sent the executed copy back to her. She opened her banking app to wire the retainer. MII was not cheap, even with their preferred friend status.

"Let's wait on the payment," he said. "There will always be time for that later, and I have no doubt that House Harrison pays their debts."

She wondered why but decided not to ask.

"How did Kitty disappear?"

Diana flicked her fingers across her tablet. "I have a video."

He pushed a card toward her with a password. She paired her tablet to the system and tapped play. The screen on the wall came to life, and the recording played across it, the sky awash with pink and lavender and a dense forest blanketing the ground, filmed from above. The familiar pines, mixed with occasional oaks and maples.

"What is this?"

"The Den. Our private lands near Sam Houston National Forest."

The woods parted, flowing around a circular clearing with a large stone building in its center.

The screen blinked and switched to a stationary security camera mounted in a tree, with the back of the structure firmly in focus, showing a reinforced gate in the center of the rear wall and a steel door next to it. The time stamp said 19:34. Dusk, just before the sun set.

The door swung open, and two people emerged.

"Aleah and Kayson," Diana said. "Our best guards."

Both of her people carried Ruger semi-auto rifles. They looked around. Aleah punched a code into the lock on the wall. Kayson took a key from his pocket, inserted it into the center bar of the gate, and turned.

"Double lock?" Augustine said. "One guard has the combination, and the other carries the key?"

She nodded.

Metal clanged. The gate swung open, and Celeste emerged onto the grass. The tigrionex moved like water. She raised her gorgeous head, her periwinkle fur rippling, and inhaled, tasting the dusk air.

The guards stood still.

The muscles of Celeste's frame contracted. She ran into the woods, bounding through the undergrowth like a teenage kitten. A moment and she vanished into the gloom pooling between the tree trunks.

"If you keep a tiger in an enclosure and feed her meat, the tiger will survive," Diana said. "She will not be happy. She may suffer from boredom and develop unchecked aggression. She could become restless and irritable. But she will live. If you confine a tigrionex and feed her the best meat in the world, she will die."

"Why?" Augustine asked.

"They must hunt. I suspect that it has to do with their digestive systems. Certain enzymes that only activate after a chase or perhaps after the hormonal burst that precedes the kill. We do not fully understand it. We supplement their diet, but primary nutrition must come from hunting. We maintain both deer and buffalo herds on our land for that purpose."

"What if she stumbles across a person?" Augustine asked.

"The property is fenced in and well protected. Cameras, alarms, guard towers. Besides, Celeste is very intelligent. She is aware of what her prey is. If a child were to blunder into her path as she is charging after a deer, she would jump over them and stay locked on her dinner."

The camera zoomed in on the two guards. They waited. Moments ticked by.

Kayson checked his watch and went back to the metal door, opened it, went inside, and reappeared with a black janitorial cart, a platform on wheels with a large metal cabinet and a trash bin attached to it. He wheeled it through the gates. Aleah looked at the woods one last time and followed him.

The view switched to the interior camera. A cozy habitat occupied a room the size of a small warehouse, grass, moss, big rocks, and fallen tree trunks under a large skylight. Two oaks spread their branches over the grass. They had built the habitat around the trees. A stream ran into a shallow pond, kept at barely a third full. Kitty could swim, enjoyed it even, and yet Diana couldn't help but worry about an accidental drowning. A shallow man-made cave rose in the corner, layered with straw. On it, a soft blue clump curled, about the size of an adult female beagle.

Kayson wheeled the cart forward and pulled a pitchfork from the rack by the wall. Aleah walked up behind him. Her arm snapped up.

Diana had watched the recording over and over. She'd nearly memorized it by now, but even so, she could barely make out the outline of the knife in the woman's hand. The blade was so small. Three inches, if that.

Aleah clamped one hand over Kayson's mouth and slit his throat. He thrashed in her grip. She let him go. Kayson stumbled forward, careened to the side, and collapsed.

She felt that cut across her own neck, like a searing wire that sliced her carotid. Diana clamped her rage and grief into an iron fist and held herself still.

On the screen, Aleah walked to the cave, picked up Kitty, slid her into a bag, lowered the bag into the metal cabinet, and wheeled the cart away.

"An illusion mage," Augustine said. "Likely a low-range Significant, possibly an upper-level Notable. Probably a woman."

Diana blinked. "How did you know?"

ON THE SCREEN, THE ASSASSIN PUSHED THE CART OUT OF THE enclosure. The view blinked, switching to the outer camera. As she turned the corner, her face blurred for the briefest of moments. She kept walking out, receding from view.

"Ah. So that's what prompted you to come to me," Augustine said. "She gave herself away."

"How did you know?" Diana repeated.

That direct stare again. How interesting. He wasn't in the habit of revealing secrets of his brand of magic, but he wanted to know her reaction.

"Most people don't realize how often they subconsciously

touch their face. We scratch our chins, brush our lips, rub our eyes... The murder victim touched his face four times. The killer didn't touch her face once. She didn't smile or raise her eyebrows. She didn't emote at all."

The industry term was "dead face." It was a sure giveaway.

"An illusion mage in disguise is acutely aware of their face at all times. Holding an illusion over stationary features is one thing. Holding it while your face moves is much harder. Every touch and every contraction of the facial muscles magnify the risk of failure."

"But why a Significant?" she asked. "I thought only Primes could produce illusions that appeared on camera."

"That's what common wisdom says. Common wisdom also states that animal mages are barely able to hold conversations and treat other people like objects."

"Yes."

"We both know that neither is exactly accurate. The other guard was important to you."

A hint of something vicious sparked in her eyes and melted. Her expression was perfectly placid the entire time, and her voice was measured and calm, even distant.

"Kayson had been with our House for ten years. He left behind a wife and an infant child. I've known Aleah since she was fourteen. She is the daughter of a long-term employee. Our House paid for her veterinary education and training. We found her in her garden. She was shot twice, in the back and in the head. She is in a medically induced coma. We don't know if she will survive."

Diana Harrison was livid. It wasn't just an insult to the House. No, these people were family, in the traditional sense of the word. She cared about them, and she buried her rage very deep inside herself. Inevitably, it would explode.

He was right to delay the payment. This was deeply

personal, and it promised to be messy and brutal. He would need plausible deniability when things turned ugly.

"My condolences," he offered.

"Thank you." She faced him. "You are right. It's not that we are unable to form attachments to people, Augustine. It's that we are conditioned to reject them."

The curiosity burned him. He had to know more. But all in good time.

Augustine nodded. "Illusion mages are the same. We take advantage of misconceptions. As does every group of magic users. Our laws require that we identify the nature of our talents, and the economic reality compels us to sort ourselves into tiers of power. Everything else is secret. Now you know one of my talent's secrets—the dead face. A sure way to identify a lower tier illusion mage in disguise."

The silence lay heavy between them.

She raised her eyebrows and wagged them.

"Yes?"

"I'm reassuring you that I'm not an illusion mage."

He almost laughed but caught himself.

"You still haven't explained your conclusions," she reminded him.

"Illusion isn't a single talent but rather a collection of abilities related to disguising oneself. They weave together like threads that make a fabric to create a different appearance. Some people are better at manifesting certain traits than others. The ability to retain an altered appearance on camera is called mirror-masking. Almost all illusion Primes and about thirty percent of Significants have it, but it sporadically occurs in people with lower power levels. Statistically, the duration of the illusion and the fact that the killer held it through the murder suggests someone who is at least a Significant, but the lack of emoting and that blur in the recording puts her in the lower range and possibly drops her down to an upper Notable."

Diana caught on fast. "And you believe that she is a woman because she would've chosen a victim of the same size to make things easier?"

"That, and the way she moved."

Explaining how he sensed that would take entirely too long. He spent most of his life observing human bodies to better imitate them, and he was rarely wrong.

"Is the ability to mimic scents an illusion skill?" she asked.

"Did the killer mimic her victim's scent?"

"She did. She passed by multiple guard dogs, and Celeste didn't sense an intruder. If her scent wasn't familiar, she would've never allowed a strange human near her den."

Augustine smiled. "That's very fortunate."

"Why?"

"Because the ability to duplicate a scent via illusion is extremely rare. That considerably narrows our suspect pool."

"Narrows it by how much?"

"There are only two families in East Texas with hypersensitivity to scents and the ability to duplicate them." He picked up his phone. "And I am going to eliminate one of them from our list."

He tapped the phone, putting the call on speaker.

"Yes, Prime Montgomery?" Marwan's voice echoed through the room.

"Where were you last night between 7:30 p.m. and 10:00 p.m.?"

"I'm still in St. Louis following the Guera case. Marina and I tailed him to RYSE and sat on him until he left at eight minutes past midnight."

"And your brother?"

"He is testifying in Boston on behalf of House Talvert. He was up half of the night doing trial prep with the ADA."

"Thank you." Augustine hung up and looked at Diana. "As

you can see, it wasn't any of mine. That leaves us with one local option. Are you sure you wish to participate?"

"Yes."

It wasn't his habit to involve the clients in the investigation. He tried his best to discourage that. However, it wouldn't be the first time the head of a House chose to attend to their problem personally. He would just have to work her presence into his plans. Besides, he had a feeling that spending time with Diana Harrison promised the kind of insight into animal mages no amount of background research could provide. Of all the magic specialties, the metamorphosis and the animal mages presented the greatest threat to his brand of power. No matter how meticulously he crafted his illusions, he couldn't alter his scent. They could identify him by smell alone. The more he knew about them, the better he could minimize that risk.

This intel would be priceless.

"Very well." Augustine pulled the keyboard to him, tapped the keys, routing the call through a series of scramblers, and typed in the number.

A dial tone sounded from the speaker. One, two...

"Yes?" The voice had a deep rasp to it.

He dialed up his magic and spoke in a bright soprano. "I have a client who wishes to meet. Two women, standard split, double rate."

"When?"

"In an hour."

"Fine."

Augustine hung up.

"Where are we going?" Diana asked.

"To visit the underbelly of Houston." He pushed the chair back and got to his feet.

"Oh. How exciting."

Diana stood up, her lips curved in a soft smile. Next to her,

the Doberman rose, too, her mouth opened in an identical
excited grin.

$$[\ 3\ ]$$

Augustine changed lanes, avoiding a slow-moving truck with landscaping equipment in the back. He'd selected a black Mercedes GLC for this trip. It was a reliable car that handled well and looked like every other crossover SUV on the road.

Diana sat in the passenger seat, calmly watching Houston roll past the window. She was carrying a small purse with her, containing her wallet and a pouch of the tigrionex milk. The dog, whose name was Lila, lay on the back seat, her head resting on her big paws. He requested to put one of their rune collars on her, and Diana agreed. The collars were the latest gadget to come out of the MII's Research and Development. The sigils inscribed on them retained a small magic charge, allowing him to affix an illusion to it. It only lasted for six minutes, but that would be long enough.

Three minutes into the drive, it occurred to him that he had talked way too much during their conversation in the office. He had told her about his sister. He had explained the particulars of illusion magic, which was the kind of proprietary knowledge any sane mage would have kept to himself. He had even disclosed the identities of his agents. She had watched him and listened, and he had just kept talking and talking.

Blah-blah-blah. Why am I chattering?

No distractions, he reminded himself. This was a job, and he was bringing a client along, a client whom he would have to protect. While Lila was a biological weapon, she was still only a dog.

The traffic on 288 was surprisingly light. Their destination lay in Pearland, about fifteen miles south of Downtown, a large suburban city within the metro. Safe, convenient, lots of restaurants, schools, and box stores.

His car chimed, announcing an incoming call. He glanced at the number and sighed.

"Yes?"

Arabella's light voice came out of the speakers. "Finished the Dunwoody thing. It's in your inbox."

"Did you find Phillip?"

"I did."

That was quick. "Where was he?"

"Stuffed into a cistern in a barn."

What? "Is he alive?"

"Yes. He had a fight with his girlfriend, was a total ass about it, and when she broke up with him, he decided to use his ice magic to keep her from leaving. She yeeted him into a cistern and then bounced. I'm surprised she was that chill about it. She showed a lot of restraint."

"Stuffing a 16-year-old into a cistern and leaving him there for two days hardly qualifies as restraint."

"It does if your last name is Madero."

Oh. "Noted."

Diana smiled.

Considering House Madero's reputation, Phillip Dunwoody was lucky to have kept all of his limbs.

"Are you still considering?" Arabella asked.

"Yes."

"What should I do next?"

"Talk to Lina. She will assign you a new case."

"Okay!"

The call ended.

"What are you considering?" Diana asked him.

"She wants to go to Rice."

Of all Texas' colleges, Rice was the best when it came to magic education. It was private, had an excellent curriculum taught by nationally recognized scholars, and kept its enrollment very small. It was also local, which was a huge plus for Arabella.

"Why can't she?" Diana asked.

"She doesn't have the grades or the pedigree for it. Even with the Path to College, her chances are slim. She is not a bad kid, and the Baylors are a loving family. Unfortunately, they have their hands full. Once they figured out that she had control over her magic, they left her to her own devices. She is independent, level-headed, and sharply intelligent, but she gets bored easily. Her grades suffer as a result."

"Independence isn't a bad quality," Diana said.

"Agreed. The problem isn't her independence. The problem is their lack of supervision. I know what my sister made on her last history exam. I'm not sure the Baylors even know what subjects Arabella is taking. She is thirty hours into her internship with MII, and I doubt anyone has asked her what she is doing with her afternoons."

Diana gazed into the distance, a contemplative look on her pretty face. "Sometimes being ignored is the better option."

His interactions with Cornelius had convinced him that childhood in House Harrison wasn't pleasant. Perhaps that was why Diana still didn't have a partner. After all, the point of Prime marriages was all about children with the right genetic makeup. She would have to choose another animal mage, and the burden to find a connection would be doubled...

And he was in the weeds again. What was it about today? He needed to get back to the subject at hand.

"Rice is very selective," Augustine said. "Low admission rate. Not only does that child want to go to Rice, but she wants to double major in Business Administration and AMT, Applied Magic Theory. She needs a letter of recommendation, and she identified me as the best sponsor. It's the reason she started this internship in the first place."

"Are you the best sponsor?" she asked.

"The dean of the AMT faculty is a family friend."

"Do you think she can do it?"

"Absolutely."

He passed another slow-moving vehicle. What was the point of getting on a state highway if you were going to sit at fifty-five?

"Then why not give her the recommendation?"

He grimaced. "Because she doesn't have the foundation for it. The Baylors have been a House for five minutes, and the AMT faculty is a shark-infested whirlpool filled with multi-generation Primes. They will rip her apart. If I give her the recommendation, I will be assuming responsibility for her, which means I will need to actually mentor her. I don't have the time, and I'm not sure I want to make the effort."

He took the exit and merged onto Sam Houston Parkway heading east. It was time. Augustine inwardly let off the imaginary brakes that held his magic back. It flowed over him and Diana, filling the car, coalescing over them and the dog, and he shaped it in a single breath with practiced ease.

The pressure lessened, and he exhaled softly.

His body generated magic at an accelerated rate. If he wasn't careful, it would erupt out of him like a geyser. Maintaining his usual persona bled some of it out, but assuming a new identity was so much better.

"Please take a moment to check your reflection," he said.

Diana flipped the sun visor on her side and looked in the mirror.

DIANA BLINKED. THE WOMAN IN THE MIRROR BLINKED WITH HER. She was middle-aged, and her blond hair, streaked with grey, was pulled into a tight bun away from her full face. The corners of her mouth and her eyes drooped slightly. Sunspots marked her cheeks, barely obscured by a thin layer of makeup. She looked tired.

Diana tilted the visor, trying to get a better view. She had acquired a larger body, dressed in a brown pantsuit.

Diana blinked again, disoriented, and tried a smile. Her reflection mimicked her.

"No worries," an elegant brunette in the driver seat said. "You can move your face."

This new woman was in her forties, her makeup expertly applied, a nude lip, razor-precision eyebrows, and that classic top-income-bracket hair, parted in the center and spilling over her shoulders in loose waves. A silk satin shirt, a grey pencil skirt. She couldn't see the shoes, but they were likely heels. At once generic and familiar, an investment banker, a luxury real estate broker, a female entrepreneur giving an interview to Forbes.

"The illusion will hold until I choose to remove it."

He didn't just look different. He sounded different. His movements were different, and yet even in this new body, he was still him. He felt like Augustine.

This was a problem. She didn't need these kinds of problems.

"What about Lila?"

The brunette nodded at the back. A large jacket lay on the seat, casually discarded.

"It would be best if she waited for us in the car," Augustine said.

"Won't the illusion break if we leave?"

"She's wearing a rune collar that acts as a short-term battery for my enchantment. We won't be long. I will leave the AC running, and once we are inside, nobody will notice."

She glanced at the overcast sky through the car window. The weather was seasonably warm for April, with highs in the mid-seventies, but today the temperature dropped to the high sixties, a luxurious cooldown. Lila would be fine with the AC.

A two-story building came into view on their right. It sat in the middle of a large parking lot, bordered by stretches of grass wide enough to be called fields. A line of trees ran behind the building. The nearest business up ahead was at least six hundred feet away or more.

Augustine slowed the Mercedes and guided it into the parking lot. She studied the structure. Two floors of sandy masonry walls with square lines and large windows. The footprint was rectangular, with the upper story slightly smaller, so it sat atop the first like the second tier of a cake. There must have been a balcony surrounding that second floor with a concrete wall acting as railing and a defensive barricade, because she could only see the top portion of the upper windows.

The first floor was large, likely around ten thousand square feet. The sign on the front spelled out "Gorwood and Associates." It looked like a no-nonsense office built in the late nineties that had been given a fresh coat of cheerfully neutral paint.

"Is this the seedy underbelly?" she asked.

"One part of it."

"I had expected something more sinister."

The brunette Augustine gave her a one-shouldered shrug. Diana could've sworn her blouse was pure silk. The temptation to check the texture made her fingertips itch.

"What is this really?" she asked him.

"A front for the Hester family. They have two Significants and a single Prime, and they're hoping to become a House."

Becoming a House was hellishly expensive. "They're trying to raise the money?" she guessed.

"By any means necessary. MII stays on the right side of the law. There are contracts that we simply won't take. The Hesters take everything. Mostly their cases involve theft, some B&E, and getting dirt for blackmail, with an occasional assassination thrown in."

"Lovely," she murmured.

"Since there is no dial-a-blackmailer service, people like the Hesters conduct their business through a series of brokers. This is Quinn Hester's secret office. He acts as the broker for the family, a seller's agent. I'm posing as Helena Lopez, also a broker, a buyer's agent."

"Am I the buyer?"

"Yes. When we're in there, please stay behind me at all times. Let me take the lead. If unusual things occur, I'll need you to step to the closest wall and stay there no matter what you see. Don't try to help me and, above all, don't run."

"Okay."

"Do I have your promise?"

"Yes."

Augustine opened the car door and stepped out. She did as well. They walked to the building side by side, Augustine's red-soled Louboutin pumps making soft clicking noises on the pavement.

Diana felt naked without her dog. She'd gotten used to an animal companion. They were a welcome buffer between her and violence. They were an effective deterrent—the fear of being bitten was a deeply ingrained human instinct.

The doors whispered open at their approach. They stepped into a simple vestibule with the polished golden oak floor and walked to the counter, where a lone receptionist sat in front of a computer screen. The place was sparsely furnished. Generic chairs, upholstered in fake leather, waited in a row by the windows between depressingly plastic trees. It could've been a doctor's office.

"How may I help you?"

"Helena Lopez," Augustine said. "We are expected."

The receptionist checked her screen. "Just a moment."

They waited. Unusual things… How interesting.

A door on the right side swung open, and a man in a cheap suit nodded to them. Augustine headed for the door, and she followed him into a short hallway. The air stank of carpet cleaner fighting with the musty odor of an old rug. They went up a flight of stairs and were ushered into a large room with no windows, a desk of polished, shiny wood, and two chairs.

A man sat behind the desk. He was in his early forties, with good bone structure, wavy dark hair, a short beard, and light grey eyes, which were complemented by his dark blue suit.

Behind him, two men stood in identical dark polo shirts and khaki cargo pants. Both were fit and muscular, with the kinds of shoulders and biceps that testified to regular hours spent at the gym. Both wore guns in the holsters on their hips. Another man, in the same business casual uniform, waited to the side.

The man who had escorted them shut the door and stood in front of it, barring their exit. Four guards, one directly to their left, one behind them, and two by the desk. With Hester, that made five against two.

Quinn Hester leaned forward and frowned. His eyebrows came together. His mouth opened. "Kill hi—"

The walls sprouted massive blisters, three feet across and

swelling like fresh burns. The one directly across from Diana ballooned, turning translucent like the membrane of some horrific amniotic sack stretched too thin, and she glimpsed something tightly coiled and moving within it. Fear slapped her, born of a deep, animal instinct.

Augustine blurred and smashed into the man to his left.

The blisters burst, releasing swirls of tentacles with suckers the size of dinner bowls. They whipped into the room, glistening, wet, contracting, and her mind shrieked at her to get away. The floor bulged, moving, as if the wood had turned into a choppy sea. Panic squirmed through her in an electric rush.

She focused on the blurry figure and took six small steps to the side.

Her shoulder hit the wall. Diana pressed her back against it.

The human blur swept to the left, leaving a limp body in his wake. He dashed by her, and she caught the faintest hint of Augustine within it, like an afterimage that instantly faded.

The blur collided with the guard by the door. Bones cracked, a guttural scream tore out, choked off in mid-note, and Augustine faded out of existence, merging with the tentacles slapping against the walls with sickening, wet thumps. The guard sprawled on the floor, unmoving.

A blister popped to her left, just inches from her head. Tentacles erupted into the room, and between them a thin tendril slithered out, a bulb on its end. The bulb turned to her and opened to reveal an eye ringed with teeth instead of eyelashes.

The guard by the door collapsed. Quinn was down to the two men by his desk. They had drawn their guns, spinning around, aiming at the revolting horrors slithering through the walls.

"Shoot!" Quinn howled and pawed at his desk.

One of the guards behind him jerked his weapon up and fired into the ceiling, where a nightmarish mouth squeezed through the fissure. It bit the air with steak-knife teeth. The other guard frantically spun around, looking around the room, trying to find Augustine among the writhing clusters of Lovecraftian flesh.

The monstrous eye continued to hover by her, watching her. Sweat drenched Diana's face, cold and sticky, as if she was sweating out her panic. This was a nightmare. Either that or she was going insane, trapped in a hallucination.

There was no scent. These terrifying things, they should have emitted an odor, and yet there was nothing except the usual smell of human bodies. She tried to hold on to that knowledge, but her mind was flailing in revulsion.

The blur popped into existence feet away from the gun-waving guard, vaulted over the desk, and slammed into him. The weapon went flying. The man folded in half, and the blur kicked out, catching the other guard in the head. The man flew into the wall and collapsed.

Quinn finally yanked a drawer open and jerked a gun out.

The blur tore into him. Quinn screamed, an awful sound filled with pain.

Everything stopped. The tentacles, the churning floor, the blur—everything disappeared. Augustine stood by the desk, holding a stocky man in his mid-twenties in an arm lock. The man was bent over the desk, his face flat against the surface. Blood seeped through his short blond hair.

Augustine's expensive suit was gone. He wore a black outfit somewhere at the crossroads between athletic warm-ups and tactical combat gear. The pants clung to his long legs, and the jacket had a short, stand-up collar, zipped up the front. The collar looked reinforced to protect his neck. The material was all slick, with nothing to grab, and close-fitting enough to cut through her alarm and fear to the part of herself that noted the swell of muscles across his biceps and chest.

The door burst open, and two more guards ran into the

room, a middle-aged man and a young man barely eighteen or so. The younger blond man grabbed for his gun.

"I wouldn't, Camden," Augustine told him, his voice ice-cold.

Camden froze, his hand on his firearm.

"Place your guns on the floor."

"Do as he says," Quinn squeezed out.

The two men placed their weapons on the cheap carpet.

"Come and join your uncle."

Camden crossed the room and stopped behind the desk. The middle-aged man followed him. Judging by their faces, all three were clearly related.

Augustine let go of Quinn, walked around the desk, and pulled out a chair, glancing at her. "Please."

He wanted her to sit. Diana willed her legs to move, walked over, and sat. He lowered himself into the other chair and threw one long leg over the other. Fabric swirled, and his expensive suit was back in place.

The three men stared at him like he was a wolf.

"I come to visit you in good faith, and you attempt to kill me," Augustine said.

"It was a misunderstanding," Quinn offered.

He was at least fifteen years younger than his initial disguise. His features had lost their refined lines. His narrow face with close-set eyes and a long chin was ordinary, neither ugly nor beautiful.

"Is it?"

"What do you want?" Quinn asked, his voice wary.

"House Harrison."

"I don't know what you're talking about."

Augustine sighed. "We're wasting time."

"We don't know anything," Camden said.

Augustine looked at her. "I was hoping to avoid it, but it can't be helped."

She saw her arms reform, her suit vanishing in an instant,

replaced by short white sleeves. The three men at the other end of the desk inhaled sharply. Camden's face contorted, his eyes turning glassy with fear.

She took her phone out and pretended to check it, hoping her expression looked sufficiently calm.

Nevada Rogan's face looked back at her through the front camera.

Oh. Wow.

"They are all yours," Augustine said to her.

"Wait!" Quinn held up his hands. "Wait, wait, wait!"

Nevada Rogan, a truthseeker. To Diana, she was a friend. To everyone else, she was the woman whose magic could wrench your most powerful secrets out of you and leave your mind broken. Diana cleared her throat, trying to remember Nevada's mannerisms.

"We didn't take the job!" Words came out of Quinn in a tumbling rush. "We turned it down. We didn't want complications. These complications."

"Who brokered it?" Augustine asked.

"Sutton. I don't know who the other broker was."

Augustine rose. "Mrs. Rogan."

She got up.

Augustine walked her to the door, held it open, and looked at the Hesters. "Next time you try to kill me will be your last."

They left the office and walked out of the building. Nobody tried to stop them.

[4]

"Augustine?"

"Yes?"

"What the fuck was that?"

Coming from her, the expletive was so unexpected, even something as common as *fuck* sounding profane. He merged onto the highway and stole a glance at Diana. The calm, slightly vapid demeanor was gone. The woman in the passenger seat was focused, like a soldier in enemy territory. He couldn't really blame her. The visit to the Hesters hadn't gone as planned.

"Do you mean the violence or the magic?"

"Yes."

Clearly some explanations were in order. He hesitated for a moment. There was no way to unpack what happened without revealing more about illusion magic than he was comfortable with. However, he had allowed her to come along, and that decision put her in danger, so the responsibility lay squarely on his shoulders.

"This is why I don't normally take clients on our investigations."

"You disarmed me by convincing me to leave Lila behind and then walked us into an ambush."

That was fair. "I apologize."

"I thought you said Quinn Hester couldn't see through your illusions?"

"He can't. Quinn is a low level Significant. Like all Hesters, he has sensitivity to smells, but it's very slight. Quinn would've bargained with me. Dealing with him is relatively straightforward. Offer enough money, and he folds. But that wasn't Quinn Hester."

"Then who was it?"

"Dylan. Their Prime. He doesn't typically get involved with the broker part of the business, but for whatever reason, Quinn wasn't there today, so Dylan took his place. I realized who he was the moment we walked in. While Dylan is on the lower end of the Prime scale, his sensitivity to smells is off the charts. He didn't see through my illusion—he sniffed me out."

"Explain the tentacles and eyes with teeth coming out of the walls."

He was hoping to avoid that, but of course, she wanted to know.

"I want to stress that this was an aberration. Had the Hesters been a House, or at least had more interactions with Houses, this would have gone much differently. Illusion Primes tend to be much more pragmatic in our interactions. We expect that other illusion Primes might come to visit us wearing a disguise. In that same situation, someone like Zaden Price would have chuckled and quipped something along the lines of, 'Prime Montgomery, fancy finding you in my office.' We would have had a much more pleasant conversation and been on our way."

"Eyes with teeth, Augustine."

Knocking her off course wasn't working.

"Please be patient. I'm getting to that. At the upper level of power, illusion mages are capable of area-of-effect alterations.

We project a dense magic field with multiple visual effects. Everyone within that range is affected. In this case, there were four armed guards and a Prime. It was essential that they be neutralized."

She was giving him a very odd look.

"When two illusion Primes fight, we attempt to shatter each other's fields. As you probably observed, an illusion mage is remarkably difficult to counter in close combat, especially when their field is active."

"I noticed," she said dryly. "You blurred and broke their bones, while they were shooting at the monster mouths biting at them from the ceiling."

"Nothing that I made could hurt them. Those were mere distractions."

"You are lying."

He glanced at her. The calm mask was back in place over her lovely features, but her voice cut like a knife.

"I was there, Prime Montgomery. My heart pounded in my chest. I tasted adrenaline in my mouth. What you created were not mere illusions. It's an alternate reality. Nightmares come to life. If I had a heart condition, I would have died. If my willpower failed, I would have hurled myself from the nearest window like the building was on fire."

He had to salvage this. "Those are temporary, secondary reactions to fear stimuli. The illusions themselves cannot touch you."

She faced him, and he glimpsed a dangerous light in her eyes. His rearview mirror showed him Lila rising in the back seat, focused on him with predatory intensity.

"They don't have to touch me. If you are unarmed, and I'm holding a gun pointed at your chest, you could kill me without lifting a finger. You could make me run into a solid wall. You could walk me off a cliff. You could herd me into traffic, or trick me into hanging myself from the power lines."

She was alarmingly perceptive. "Technically true, but I would be much more likely to simply disarm you."

He regretted it as soon as he said it. It only confirmed her words.

"And then I would be at your mercy."

The things that he imagined doing with Diana at his mercy... The world screeched to a sudden halt.

He slammed that mental door shut. He would deal with that surprise thought detour later. Right now, he had to smooth this over.

There were layers to illusion, and the most essential of them had nothing to do with magic, but with controlling how you were perceived. His father's words surfaced from his memory: *Appear as an accomplished manager, project competence befitting the CEO of MII, but never permit them to learn your combat capabilities. They must see you as a business partner, proficient but obsessed with perfection and vanity. Show as little of your true self as possible. Make them think that illusion is all you have. Your life depends on it.*

Augustine had structured his public image around this tenet. He had altered his daily appearance, policed his interactions with even his closest allies, and taken his ego out of it—and, for the most part, he'd accomplished his goal. When people evaluated his threat potential, they defaulted to his illusions. Their worst fear was that he might enter their lives in a disguise and ferret out some crucial secret. He had convinced them that if his illusions ever failed, he would be helpless.

Fucking Dylan Hester. His fingers tightened around the wheel on their own. He should've broken a few bones while he'd had his hands on him. Unfortunately, Diana had been there.

He'd caught the look on her face just as he bent Dylan over the table. He'd expected fear or confusion. He hadn't seen any of that. What he'd witnessed was much more disturbing. She went flat. Not just expressionless. Flat. It was as if her ego had receded deep into her psyche, and what it left behind wasn't altogether human. She'd stared at him, unblinking. No emotion. No thinking. Just this eerie presence that was aware and watching his every move. Her reaction had tripped some sort of instinctual alarm ingrained in his very DNA, the kind of visceral recognition of danger that guaranteed you ran away from a tiger. It made him stop and reconsider.

"Why did Dylan try to kill you?" she asked.

Because he is a nervous fool.

"Dylan panicked. The moment he figured out who I was, he reacted without thinking. He has no reason to kill me. We are not in competition. The Hesters don't have the resources to take our kind of contracts, and we have no reason to do the high-risk jobs they specialize in. We are not in a feud. In fact, our prior interactions were forceful but cordial."

"What does that mean?"

It meant that, last time, he'd walked into the Hesters' HQ pretending to be their mother, walked around for half an hour, then shed his disguise in the middle of the family dinner, and explained the terms of their continued operation in MII territory. Super-sensitivity to scents had its limits, especially when a strong enough perfume was involved.

"We had a business meeting, during which we established boundaries."

She shook her head. Diana would never see him the same way. His carefully structured disguise had been dealt a fatal blow. He'd had no choice—low-end or not, Dylan was a Prime. Neutralizing him had been a priority. He should've never taken her along for it.

"Why didn't Dylan recognize Nevada as another illusion?" she asked.

Sigh. "Lack of combat experience. In Dylan's place, I would have attacked you. Or shot me. Instead, he sank all of his power into trying to break my illusion field. By the time I pinned him, he was completely spent. It takes a lot of magic and a concerted effort to pierce one of my illusions. He simply wasn't strong enough, and he exhausted himself."

Diana didn't respond.

This really could have gone better. He had an irrational urge to turn the car around, drive back to the Hesters' brokerage, and punch some walls with Dylan's face.

"Augustine?"

They were back on a first name basis. He felt tension drain from him. Curious how he hadn't realized he'd been holding it. "Yes, Diana?"

"Can all illusion Primes do that?"

"Define 'that'?"

"Don't be obtuse. Can all illusion Primes create area illusions like you?"

He had to dodge this one. "To a lesser degree."

"Do you know any other illusion mages who are as strong as you?"

"That is outside the scope of this investigation. We are looking for a specific kind of illusion mage, and that mage is unlikely to match me in power."

"You didn't answer my question."

"I could answer it, but you're asking for House-specific intelligence, and it would be very expensive."

"You're a monster," she murmured.

He blinked, sure he'd misheard. She'd said it like a compliment.

She asked, "Where are we going now?"

"To visit Sutton."

"He was the broker who arranged the theft."

He nodded. "Sutton is the seller's agent. He specializes in blind deals. He doesn't know any particulars. He doesn't know who the client is, because he only works with brokers. You tell him what kind of specialist you want to hire, and he finds the right candidate and connects the two of you together. He collects an introduction fee and leaves it at that. Whether or not an agreement is reached matters not at all to him."

If she understood correctly, Sutton knew two things: the name of the buyer's broker and the name of the thief. She was almost certain that the culprit behind the theft was a Prime, and any broker that worked with Primes would be well protected and difficult to reach. Besides, they didn't have a lot of time.

No, it was much easier to go after the thief.

"What should I brace myself for? The undead? Krakens? Colossal gelatinous globs hungry for human flesh?"

"Nothing like that, I assure you. Sutton and my family go way back. I do not anticipate any problems."

"I'm bringing my dog," she informed him. "Don't try to talk me out of it."

"Wouldn't dream of it," he promised.

SUTTON MADE HIS LAIR IN A SIXTEEN-STORY OFFICE TOWER ON Augusta Drive, right in the middle of the crowded cluster of retail, office, and apartment buildings that had sprung up around the Galleria. The mall billed itself as "Texas' largest and most luxurious shopping destination," and the resulting labyrinth of commercial property around it was its own busy, dense microcosm.

Augustine parked in the back lot, exited the car, and held her door open.

He was back in his perfect businessman persona. Not a single strand of pale gold hair out of place. No damage on his knuckles. There was no way to tell how much of it was illusion, but she didn't smell blood on him.

She'd taken a good look at the bodies sprawled on the floor on her way out. They looked broken. He'd put four guards in the hospital. She was amazed they hadn't heard an ambulance wail as they drove out.

This man was utterly terrifying. And he was holding open her door. A frisson of alarm dashed along her nerves. It was delicious.

Diana stepped out of the vehicle.

Augustine then opened the rear passenger door, and she sent a light push along the bond to Lila. The dog jumped out and took her usual position by Diana's side. The familiar feedback of Lila's emotions trickled in through the bond: happiness, anticipation, curiosity, and a slight tinge of eagerness. Lila was a young dog, conditioned to be a bodyguard. She had personally trained Lila to respond to immediate threats and to make her own judgements. The Doberman lacked the single-minded drive of some police canines who started whining as soon as they saw a suspect, anticipating the chase and the release of the bite. But she had spent a long time in the car. Lila was looking forward to a bit of exercise.

They crossed the parking lot, aiming for the entrance. All of Diana's senses were dialed up, keyed to Augustine striding at her side. She noted everything in detail: the way he moved, the way he placed his feet and shifted his weight, his breathing, his scent… Her memory reproduced that dark suit, the contours of hard muscle stretching the dark fabric.

She didn't have to do anything about it, she reminded herself. Acknowledging it was enough.

"Who will I look like this time?" She'd managed to keep her voice light.

"Yourself."

"No disguise?"

He shook his handsome head. "There will be no need. Sutton understands the way the game is played. He's a professional."

"Augustine?"

"Yes?"

"If I wasn't there, would you have killed all of them?"

There was a tiny pause before he answered. "It would've been bad for business."

Lila let out a tiny woof. Diana sent a reassuring flood of calm down the link. *Yes. Spectacular, isn't he?*

They entered the lobby and took the elevator to the eighth floor. It released them into a hallway with a small reception area. The colors were brown and beige. A row of square canvas paintings lined the wall, depicting thin abstract swirls the color of cinnamon on eggshell backgrounds.

A man in his early twenties sat behind the desk, typing away on the keyboard. He was redheaded, with a pale face and thick glasses, and when he turned away from the screen, he smiled.

"Hello, can I help you?"

"Montgomery for Sutton," Augustine said.

"One moment." The receptionist picked up his cell and texted.

His phone clicked, announcing an incoming message.

"Please go ahead," the man said.

Augustine turned to the left. They walked down the hallway to the third door on the right. He knocked and swung it open, not bothering to wait for an answer.

The office was large and dim. Heavy green curtains blocked the sunlight. A cheap, mass-produced rug in matching green sheathed the floor. In the middle of the room, a single desk of dark wood supported a laptop and a simple table lamp. One chair behind it, two in front. No bookshelves, no plants, no decorations.

A man sat behind the desk. Her eyes adjusted to the low light, and she could pick up on his features now. He was in his sixties, with a broad frame, made even wider by the cut of his dark suit. His silver hair and white beard contrasted with his bronze skin, and his maroon glasses frames matched the plum color of his dress shirt.

Lila hesitated. A trickle of unease dripped down their mental link. Something was wrong with the room.

Augustine shut the door, walked up to the chairs, and held one out for her. She sat. Lila lowered herself next to her, sitting on her haunches. He took the other chair.

"Prime Montgomery," Sutton said quietly.

The other man seemed relaxed. No apprehension in his eyes, no tension in the pose, no excessive sweating. And yet there was something about him that felt off.

"Sutton."

Diana focused on Sutton, sinking into a deep, calm place. In her mind, a thick tree limb formed above the room. She sat on it, watching herself and the two men from above, letting her senses take in the room, process the cues, and identify the wrongness.

Sutton looked at her. "And who might this be?"

Augustine didn't answer.

"She looks like Prime Harrison. Not a bad choice, all things considered." Sutton squinted at her. "Given the friendship pact, it makes perfect sense. But who is that really under the mask?"

Augustine ignored him. "I'm looking for a contractor."

The wrongness congealed. She could feel it better now. It had a definite direction, stretching across the room. She sank even deeper into that calm place where human emotions fell away, and the world was reduced to simple needs. *Hunger. Thirst. Safety. Augustine.*

Her attention snagged on him, on his body, on the way he sat. His scent slipped past her, waiting to be sampled. Mmmm.

"You know how I feel about discretion," Sutton said.

"I also know how you feel about adequate compensation."

"For a man of your resources, adequate won't do."

He was shaking Augustine down, the human part of her noted. She didn't like that. A hint of danger pricked her, driving her instincts into combat sharpness.

"I'd say, for you, the compensation would have to be at least generous," Sutton said.

The wrongness snapped all the way into focus, and she saw it, thin filaments of magic stretching across the room, with Sutton at their center like a spider. Animals instinctually sensed magic, and right now she was more animal than not. More than that, she was a Prime. She felt the magic, saw it, heard it... On its own, none of those senses would've been enough, but combined with her power, they formed a complete picture.

One of Sutton's tendrils spiraled up her chair. Another had made its way to Augustine, hovering just short of touching. And the third had wrapped around Lila's throat. The dog felt it, but her training kept her still.

She leaped, landing on the table in a crouch and pressed her knife against Sutton's throat. The filamentor held still. Lila snapped to her feet.

"Release my dog." Her voice was low and devoid of emotion, a growl of a predator defending her domain.

The filaments recoiled.

Augustine rose and offered his hand to her. She took it. He put his other hand on her waist, and she let him lift her off the table to her feet. The brief contact with his body sent a shiver through her.

Like touching a live wire. Being close to Augustine was its own kind of ache, exquisite in a way, a promise broken before it was ever made.

She squashed the urge to stretch herself against him. Sinking that deep into her inner self was a mistake. It lowered inhibitions. Reasserting control would require a lot of effort.

"In heels," Sutton said. "Impressive."

Augustine let her go, and her entire body mourned.

Diana forced herself to sit and stroked Lila's velvet head. The Doberman sat back on her haunches.

"You're an assassin."

"I was, at one time," Sutton confirmed.

Filamentors wove webs of arcane energy. Unlike the mages who worked with metal wires, they didn't kill directly. Their filaments syphoned off energy, draining their target until they fell into a stupor and killing them became child's play.

It made sense. A retired killer-for-hire would have the contacts required to become a broker.

"As I told you last time, curiosity is a vice for someone in your profession," Augustine said to him.

He'd moved behind her and remained standing. She was acutely aware of his fingers resting on the chair's back, close to her neck on either side. Another little thrill. She had to stop reacting.

"Sadly, I can't help myself. You said you were looking for a contractor?"

"An illusion mage. Scent-sensitive."

"And not a Hester," Sutton guessed.

"No," Augustine said.

He wasn't even asking about the other broker. Like her, Augustine must've decided that the thief was their best option.

"I want a favor," Sutton said.

"What kind?" Augustine asked.

If she stretched her neck and rubbed her cheek on his right wrist, he probably wouldn't take it well. But it was so tempting. She could have shifted away from him, but she stayed where she was. She'd never thought of herself as a masochist, so why did she keep looking for the pain of having him near and not being able to touch?

"I don't know yet," Sutton said.

What were they even talking about? She toyed with her

knife and tried to recapture the severed string of the conversation. Something, something... Compensation. Favor. Sutton wanted a favor.

"You asked for generous compensation, not munificent," Augustine said.

"And you are asking me to break confidentiality. You're not looking for an illusion mage but for *the* illusion mage, the one I'd found two weeks ago. If people found out that I've talked, I would have a hard time staying in business."

"I doubt that," Augustine said.

"I will grant you a favor," she said.

She instantly regretted it. The impulse to act had been too strong, so she redirected it, and she'd done it badly.

"Diana," Augustine murmured, a cautious note in his voice.

"A favor from Prime Harrison," Sutton said, nearly singing the words. "Yes, that will do."

"There are conditions to that favor," Augustine said. "Nothing that will endanger her and hers directly. No wet work, no police involvement."

Wise. She preferred to avoid the police, and murder always carried consequences.

"Agreed." Sutton offered her his hand across the table. "Shake on it."

She focused on his fingers, checking for the filaments, found none, and gripped his hand. They shook.

"Juliana Glass," Sutton said.

"Why does that sound like a pseudonym?" Augustine said.

"It's a stage name. She is a stuntwoman. Usually operates out of Vancouver, but she is shooting a film at HCS."

Diana raised her eyebrows.

"Hill Country Studios," Augustine clarified. "Half an hour south of Austin."

Hill Country. She knew the area. Limestone and granite

hills, narrow ravines, caves, all of it dry, rocky, and sheathed in drought-resistant shrubs.

Sutton smiled at her. "Happy chase, Prime Harrison. One hunter to another."

She slipped off the chair, slid the knife back into her thigh sheath, walked to the door, and paused half a breath for Augustine to open it. They stepped into the hallway and walked down the corridor toward the reception and elevators.

"That was unwise," Augustine murmured.

"We're running out of time."

A teenage girl with ginger hair and a splattering of freckles on her face turned the corner ahead, walking toward them. She was about fifteen or so, dressed in ripped jeans and a white off-the-shoulder blouse.

Augustine stopped.

The teenager grinned. Her face split, revealing an old East Asian woman, then a goth-looking white man with dyed black hair, and then finally a Black man in his thirties, clean-shaven, with a short haircut and intense dark eyes. An elegant grey suit clasped his lean frame, and a double golden hoop twinkled in his right ear.

"Zaden," Augustine greeted him.

"Augustine."

Someone like Zaden Price would have chuckled and quipped something along the lines of...

"Imagine finding you here of all places." He smiled, but his face remained focused, his eyes fixed on them both, searching for weakness, evaluating them as targets.

Her instincts wailed in alarm.

"Needs must," Augustine said.

"Ortega?" Zaden asked.

"Not at all," Augustine said. "A private House matter."

The intensity of Zaden's stare eased a little. He gave her a slight, self-mocking bow. His voice gained a smooth overtone. "Prime Harrison."

"Prime Price," she said.

"You know my name. I'm truly flattered. Perhaps we will see more of each other going forward."

"Perhaps not," Augustine told him.

Zaden grinned. His body spun, like a piece of paper twisting into a spiral, and the red-headed teenager was back. She gave them a long look and squeaked in a high-pitched voice. "That suit is mid, Augustine. It's giving beta. Later!"

She sauntered down the hallway toward Sutton's office.

Augustine sighed and turned toward the elevator. They were out in the parking lot, before Diana said, "*I* like your suit. It goes with your eyes."

"Thank you," he told her.

"Since he was pretending to be a teenage girl, he had to read you. It's in the job description."

The murderous demigod smiled, opened the rear passenger door for Lila, and then held the car door open for Diana. "No worries. I'm secure in my rizz."

She slipped inside and buckled her seat belt. He got behind the wheel and guided the car onto the street.

"Helicopter?" she asked.

He nodded. "It's a forty-five-minute flight."

MII had access to a military helicopter. Nice. "From the MII building?"

"Yes."

She tapped her phone. "Gerardine? I need Akela and Whiskey at MII. Please bring my work clothes and a new pouch."

"Understood," Gerardine murmured.

Diana hung up.

Augustine threw her a curious look

"Backup," she said. "The hills are wooded, and it will be evening by the time we get there."

He didn't respond. Diana settled into her seat and took a long breath. Kayson's face shimmered, rising from the depths of her memory. Fury bit her with scalding teeth.

A hunt was coming. Finally, a chance to bleed off all the rage, grief, and frustration.

About time.

[5]

A row of townhouses sat nestled between the hill in the back and the parking lot, shaded by live oaks. Behind the first hill, other slopes rose, their spines sheathed in more oaks, mountain cedar with hairy bark, pecan, and mesquite. Big, pitted chunks of limestone littered the dry, rugged terrain like natural landmines.

Diana inhaled the evening air. It smelled of cedar, strong and itchy. Ugh. At least it wasn't the cedar pollen season.

True to form, the MII helicopter was everything Augustine implied it would be. It was fast, safe, and too loud for a conversation. They didn't speak, so she concentrated on keeping Akela and Whiskey calm and read the files he'd forwarded to her tablet.

Juliana Glass' real name was Kensley Hicks. She was thirty years old, born in Vernal, Utah, and registered as a lower range Significant illusion mage. Her professional record was a series of positions with various illusion Houses, all of which had eventually cut her loose. For the past six years, she had been self-employed. According to Augustine's sources, she was a person of interest in two murder investigations and would've been arrested in a third one, had the investigation not collapsed due to police misconduct.

Kensley Hicks was a hired killer. Her wet work provided her with a comfortable lifestyle. She owned a mansion in Utah. Six million, paid outright, in a cash deal. Augustine's team had found pictures online. Diana scrolled through them, looking at an enormous white house with a backdrop of snow-capped mountains. The gallery of images rolled under her fingertips, their captions announcing the blood-soaked luxury. Twelve thousand square feet, a private gym, an indoor pool, spa, movie theater, white picket fences with horses grazing in the pasture... Diana kept thinking of Aleah in the hospital bed, wrapped in a tangle of wires and tubes, and Kayson's wife, her dark eyes red with tears, hugging Kayson's body to herself and rocking gently back and forth...

They had landed just before seven behind a warehouse building. A car was already there, waiting for them, a GMC Yukon in a boring anonymous grey. A woman waited by it. She was young, fit, and had a no-nonsense air about her. Augustine approached, she passed the key to him, turned, and walked away.

Augustine held the door open for Akela and Whiskey. She settled the wolves in, noting that the third row of seats had been removed. Instead, a large crate of black plastic occupied all available cargo space, rising just high enough to keep from obstructing the view through the rear window.

Augustine got behind the wheel. The four of them traveled past the massive studio lots and took a side road that carried them behind the sound stages, deeper into the Texas hills, where several enclaves of temporary housing sprouted among the slopes like mushrooms from a mossy forest floor.

They spoke little on the way. She'd sunk into herself, too obsessed with the prospect of the hunt, and he must've sensed it because he stayed silent. Now they had parked before the row of townhouses, small two-story units, each with a balcony and identical door, with the siding painted in shades of beige and olive green.

It would be twilight soon.

"Which unit?" she murmured.

"12B." He nodded at the last townhome on the right.

"Shall we knock?"

"I think that would be best."

They got out of the Yukon. She had no idea what she looked like, but her legs were clad in jeans, so an illusion was in place. She'd changed before getting into the MII helicopter. She wore her hunting clothes now, a pixelated camo tracksuit and running shoes. The fresh pouch of Celeste's milk was resting in the oversized pocket of her jacket, being kept warm by her body heat.

Next to her Augustine was the picture of a young Austin professional: a blue polo shirt, khaki cargo pants. He'd lost ten years and four inches of height and gained fifteen pounds. His face turned round, with brown stubble and wavy dark hair brushed back, a broad nose, and a wide smile.

She glanced down where two French bulldogs trotted by her, one tan and the other black. He'd changed their appearances, but he could do nothing about their gait. They stalked forward, paw over paw. The black Frenchie raised his muzzle to the sky and inhaled, sampling the scents. His lips trembled.

She would've laughed if she wasn't so focused on their target.

They approached the unit. Augustine raised his hand to the door.

Feedback flooded her, flowing through the bond from Akela: the sound of the wind through the window in the back, the scent growing fainter, the lack of sound.

"She's gone." Her voice was a low growl, and she didn't care.

"What?"

"She fled."

The illusion dropped without warning, and the two bulldogs vanished, revealing two grey wolves, one white and the other a dark grey.

Their bonds strummed with magic. The wolves had caught the scent trail. She dove into the bond. It was like jumping head-first into a swift river. The magic current pulled her until the line between her and the wolves blurred and they became a group, a whole. A pack.

The trail ignited before her mental vision—a glowing, ragged thread leading up, into the overgrown hills.

Akela raised his head. His eyes burned into her. Whiskey shivered with anticipation.

Go!

She sprinted across the parking lot, running at full speed.

"Diana!" Augustine screamed.

She leaped over the curb and rocks and dashed into the brush. The two wolves darted ahead, weaving between the trees. Oaks and cedars flew by. Her muscles warmed, turning loose and pliant. Her world expanded, her ears catching distant sounds, her eyes registering the flickers of life among the trees. Odors flooded the trail, pushing in from all sides: the nutty, fir-tinted signature of squirrels, the musty, old-gym-bag stink of raccoon, the sharp tang of a female mountain lion, the rats, the rabbits, the birds…

She sent commands down the bonds to the wolves. At this distance, this close, she didn't even have to whisper.

Silent, quiet, hidden. Track.

The thread shone brighter. They were gaining on their target.

The wolves crested the hill and plunged into the ravine below, and she followed, so light on her feet, she was nearly flying. She jumped over ragged chunks of limestone, dodged trees, and slipped through the brush, fast and sure. There would be no backup. No human could match her speed, not in this terrain with twilight creeping in. If Augustine tried, he would break his legs.

That was perfectly fine. This was a family matter.

They crossed the shallow valley and started up another hill. The trail vibrated, solidifying. The thread was solid now, like a fluid glowstick, veering between the tree trunks. Her enhanced hearing caught the rapid thumps of feet in boots striking the ground. Their prey was near.

She pushed a command down the bond. The wolves split, darting to the sides. They bounded uphill. A slight burn nipped at her legs, the first sign of fatigue. She dismissed it and kept running, pushing up the rocky slope.

The air flung a new scent at her, the foul, rotting, nauseating stench of putrid vomit. Llama spit. They were likely passing by a ranch.

The trail faltered, dimming and diffusing into the stench. Kensley had realized she was being tracked and was trying to disguise her trail.

Diana almost laughed.

The wolves slowed, padding through the chaotic violence of the llama spit. The solid glowing line of the trail had turned into a faint cloud, but the two hundred and eighty million olfactory receptors in wolf noses had given them the kind of sensitivity the human body couldn't overcome. They sorted through the llama scents, picked the one that didn't quite fit the pattern, and were off again.

Within moments, the trail solidified back into a solid glow, then changed slightly. A different human scent—Kensley, altering her signature again. It didn't matter. Both Akela and Whiskey had locked on, and the three of them chased the glowing line through the clump of cedars up the slope and to the left.

The ground leveled out again. She caught a flash of a clearing through the trees, a group of live oaks, thick and twisted, with a dozen trunks growing from almost the same spot, rising up, then curving nearly parallel to the ground.

The flicker of black was her only warning. Diana darted behind a cedar trunk just as the gun barked twice. Bullets bit into the other side of the tree, but she was already moving, slinking along the rocky terrain on all fours with inhuman speed, past the thicket of agarita to the left. A few more feet, and Diana sank to the ground, hidden by a mountain laurel bush, and went still.

In front of her, the massive live oak rose from the hillside. Someone had cleared the brush around it, and the packed-gravel ground lay bare. A stone bench—just a slab of limestone resting on two other chunks—waited by the tree, and beyond it, there was a hole of open air. Kensley had run to a scenic over-look near the apex of the hill.

Diana inhaled deeply. Her senses sampled the environment and identified the foreign presence, a shadow figure leaning against the big oak's trunk. The assassin had tried to blend in, weaving an illusion, but she was not nearly as skilled as Augustine. She had succeeded in matching the color and pattern of her clothes, skin, and hair to the oak's bark, but she was still human-shaped. She still breathed and smelled, although she had altered her scent again, trying to match the cedar. In her place, Augustine would've been invisible.

Diana held still and listened to the soft whisper of air going in and out of Kensley's nose.

Her bond told her Akela had circled all the way to the back. He was ten yards behind the woman, while Whiskey crouched on Diana's right, not too far from the direction from which they had originally come.

The wolves waited, and she waited with them. She had waited this long; she could wait a little longer.

Minutes passed, soft and slow. The sun was setting, and the golden and pink light of the sunset was dying slowly, congealing into dusk.

Kensley shifted by the trunk.

More moments, falling down softly like feathers, marked by Kensley's breaths.

The killer took a slow step from behind the trunk, holding her gun with both hands.

Diana leaned forward, the muscles of her legs flexing, compacting herself like a panther just before it leaped.

Her magic found a red-tailed hawk in a treetop across the clearing. She wasn't as compatible with birds as Cornelius, but she didn't need much.

The hawk flew with a screech.

Kensley spun toward the noise, firing two shots in the direction of the sound.

Diana pounced.

She launched herself out of the brush, clearing the distance in a single bound. Her weight landed on Kensley's back, and Diana locked her hands on the illusion mage's neck and yanked her backward. Kensley's legs folded under her. She dropped, trying to roll and bring the gun around, but Diana ripped it out of her hand and threw it. The weapon went flying. Diana let go and bounced away.

Not yet. That would have been too quick.

Kensley jumped to her feet. Her eyes went right, then left, looking for an escape.

Akela and Whiskey emerged from the brush. Whiskey's golden eyes glowed, catching the last rays of daylight. Akela's lips trembled in the beginning of a snarl. He showed his fangs, long and white.

Kensley's eyes went wide. There it was. Fear. Delicious, sweet fear.

Be afraid, Kensley. Be more afraid.

The wolves took a step. Another.

Diana could see the calculation in her eyes. Two wolves or one human.

Kensley charged her, aiming to knock her off-balance. Diana met her halfway. Her hand closed on Kensley's neck and she fell backward, planting her right foot just above the assassin's hip. Kensley's momentum carried her up and over. Her back slammed the ground. The air burst out of Kensley's mouth.

For a fraction of a second, they were both on their backs, heads toward each other. Diana flipped over, her hands on the ground, her feet digging into the gravel, as if she were a sprinter crouched in the starting position. She surged forward, looming over Kensley. She knew exactly what the other woman saw: her face, shadowed in twilight, her teeth bared, and her eyes glowing with eerie, golden magic. The color of the glow shifted depending on its intensity, green when her power was a trickle, yellow when it was a river, and right now she was all in.

Kensley sucked in a hoarse breath and Diana slapped her across the face. The blow knocked Kensley to the side. A little harder, and she could have broken her neck.

Not yet.

Kensley scrambled to her feet and leaped as Whiskey bit the air an inch from her thigh. The assassin spun around, her eyes wild and drowning in terror.

There it was, the scent of true fear, spiced with adrenaline, flavored with cold sweat, accented with a rapid heartbeat. Diana let it wash over her and drank it in. Akela raised his gorgeous head and howled, singing a long blood-curdling song that promised pain and death.

"It wasn't personal," Kensley stammered. "It was just a job."

Diana tilted her head, watching her. There was a gap

between Diana and Whiskey, ten feet of clear space that led to the slope down the hill. It was Kensley's only chance.

"It wasn't—"

Kensley charged, her hand swinging in a punch, aiming at Diana's face. A distraction, designed to force her to shy back, opening the way to escape.

Diana caught Kensley's wrist, pulled her forward and hammered a vicious sidekick into the assassin's ribs.

Bone crunched.

Diana let go, and Kensley staggered back, clutching her side with a whimper. Her first deep breath would be pure agony, and the pain on her face was intoxicating.

Diana stalked toward her.

Kensley spun, trying to run, but Diana was faster. Grasping her shoulder and pulling her backwards while sweeping her legs out from under her was child's play. Kensley's back hit the ground, and Diana landed on top of her, her knee resting on the exact spot her foot had connected with.

Kensley howled, a scream ragged with pain.

Diana pulled her knife.

The assassin's eyes focused on the blade. She struck at Diana, aiming for her throat. Diana knocked the blow aside, pinned her arm to the ground, and thrust the knife into her shoulder joint.

Another hoarse scream. Kensley's right arm was a useless lump of human flesh. Diana raised her knife.

"Adrian Woodward!" Kensley groaned. "It was Woodward. He wanted the creature. He wants to make a construct out of it. He was very specific. It needed to be alive and delivered today, because he is flying in this evening. He's going to kill it tonight to see what's inside it. He needs to know how it works."

Diana gripped Kensley's throat.

"Canyon Lake," Kensley croaked. "Compound. I can show you… It wasn't personal. Just a job."

"You hurt my family. You killed. You stole. You made orphans." The magic sang in Diana's voice, ancient like the howl of a wolf and the snarl of a panther.

"Please. Please. I will do anything."

"Bring Kayson back."

Kensley stared at her, her eyes bottomless with horror.

Diana's knife sliced.

[6]

Augustine tripped on another fucking rock and killed a curse before it escaped his mouth. He'd been stumbling through the brush, half blind with the darkness closing in. It was ungodly hot, more fucking hot than it had any right to be in April, and there was no trail. Just jagged chunks of limestone, thorny bushes, and clumps of trees that looked starved of water. This place was a barren shithole, and he forced his way through it, not knowing if he was going the right way or if he'd been walking in circles.

He'd heard gunshots fifteen minutes ago. They'd rolled through the hills, a twin burst of sound that came from everywhere, echoing through the scrub, then another pair of shots a few moments later. He'd tried to aim for the direction he thought the shots had originated. It took him up another hill, and then, a short time later he heard a howl. Some deeply buried part of him recognized it wasn't a coyote. No, that was something bigger. A threat that resonated through his spine, and he hated the way it made him feel. And then he went toward it.

He ran most days, a standard warm-up before a regimen of

weights and sparring. He knew he was in superb shape, and yet this damn hill felt like it would end him.

Diana had shot through it like she had wings. He had expected her to sic the wolves and follow. But he did not expect her to charge up the wooded hillside at the speed of an Olympic sprinter. How the fuck did she do that?

He had been expecting something like this to happen since the moment she jumped from her chair straight onto Sutton's desk and put a knife to his throat. But he didn't expect *that*. She bounded up that fucking hill like she was a metamorphosis Prime, except she did not transform. She just ran.

Nothing in his research said that animal mages gained any kind of enhanced capabilities. Was it just the Harrisons, or was everything he knew about animal mages catastrophically wrong? He needed to solve this damn mystery, the sooner the better.

Augustine pushed his way through the brush, wincing at the thorns catching on his clothes. A massive tree rose before him, a clump of trunks curving from it like some giant, gnarled version of a monstera plant done in oak. It jutted from the spine of the hill, ruling over a stretch of clear ground. He registered a body by its roots and two huge wolves sitting beside it. They looked at him. He noted the blood staining their mouths. It should have alarmed him, but there was a bigger threat, and she commanded all of his attention.

She lay sprawled on the curving trunk, twenty-five feet above the ground, a lithe, graceful creature with glowing golden eyes. Her hair had come loose, and it spilled over her shoulders, framing her face. She watched him step out from the brush with predatory focus, and when he met her gaze, it sent a shudder through him.

Augustine froze.

She was beautiful and terrifying. More than human. He'd read myths, part of a well-rounded education, where people ventured into the wilderness and found something there, something so mystical, powerful, and incomprehensible, they made names for it. Dryads, Huldras, gods. He didn't know what she was, but she was one of those.

The wolves ignored him and went back to their prey.

He knew he had to say something, do something, but instead he stood, petrified, and stared. If he moved, he would become prey. His body was certain of it. His instincts screamed at him, warning that she could leap off that branch and be on him in an instant. He wouldn't be able to stop it, and he wasn't sure he would try.

She stretched, like a great cat, and slipped down the trunk, landing softly on her feet. It was the hottest thing he had ever seen. She walked toward him, and it was liquid sex. He swallowed, aware he'd gone hard.

She stopped three feet from him. He was still afraid to move, not scared for his life but terrified that this would end.

"Adrian Woodward," she said. Her voice was a low purr.

The words didn't register. They just bounced off his deluded brain.

"Augustine."

He liked the way she said his name. He wanted her to say it again. To moan it.

"Augustine! Focus."

If she touched him, he would haul her up against the tree and fight the wolves if they tried to stop him.

"Prime Montgomery!"

The words finally penetrated the haze in his brain like a cold rush of water. He made his mouth move. "Yes?"

"Adrian Woodward has my cub. He's going to dissect her tonight. His compound is somewhere in Canyon Lake."

He pulled his cellphone out, tapped it, and spoke into it on autopilot. "Get me everything on Adrian Woodward."

He ended the call and stared at her.

"Take your rabbit," Diana said over her shoulder.

The two wolves ripped a small bloody carcass in half and trotted toward them.

"They were too excited after the hunt," she told him.

He shook his head, trying to fling away the last vestiges of whatever spell she'd cast on him. "I thought ..."

"It's not good for them to feed on humans. It sets a bad precedent. Follow me. It's almost dark, and we need to get back to the car."

He trailed her down the slope, trying desperately to reassert some kind of self-control. All of his fail-safes, all of the self-imposed conditioning that had carried him through the kind of missions that would have broken him otherwise, she had smashed through all of them. For a moment, there were no restraints. The failure of his willpower shook him to his core. It was profound.

He had to get a grip. She was a client, this was a case, she was a friend of his House... If he didn't start thinking with the head that mattered, both of them would be dead, because Adrian Woodward was a Prime.

Woodward.

Unfinished business that came back to haunt him.

The problem with allowing a group of people with unrivaled individual power to police themselves was obvious. Sooner or later, some of them would stop playing by the rules and attempt to consolidate all power into their own hands. The magic elite were no different.

A few years ago, some Houses formed an alliance seeking to upend the social order and usurp the authority of the Texas State Assembly, a body that governed the conduct of magic users in the state. That alliance became known as the Conspiracy, and its goal had been to restructure the republic into an empire, with a Caesar-like figure at the top and Primes enjoying unlimited privileges.

Rogan, the Baylors, and the Harrisons opposed it, forming their own alliance. Augustine had been drawn into it. No, he'd thrown himself into it despite valid and logical reservations, because he would not tolerate tyranny. No matter how lofty the pretend goals or high-sounding the rhetoric, the true face of the Conspiracy was ugly and brutal. It sought to be a totalitarian regime with Primes at the top, and he fought them with all the savagery he possessed. He'd been idealistic once, and he thought that part of him had died, until something inside him stood up and refused to be an accessory to the murder of democracy.

Woodward had been a part of the Conspiracy. The evidence of his involvement was circumstantial but compelling. Woodward was an animator. He crafted elaborate constructs made of metal, plastic, and wire and infused them with magic, bringing them to life. Every animator had a signature, and Woodward's was obvious. His constructs looked like monstrous animals.

A construct attacked Rogan after he had delivered a vital piece of evidence to the Harris County DA. It had been guided by a powerful animator who wore a Zeta Sigma Mu ring, exclusive to members of an elite, magic-users-only fraternity. Woodward ticked all the boxes—he was a Prime animator, he lived in the area, his history had suggested that he wouldn't hesitate to attack the DA office or another Prime, and he wore the ring. He had been the Treasurer of the Dartmouth Chapter during his college days.

Augustine had zeroed in on Woodward quickly, but despite MII's best efforts, he failed to obtain conclusive proof. It ate at him, but at the time he could do nothing about it.

Then, Woodward popped up again, a year later, when Rogan, the Baylors, and the Harrisons united to take down Alexander Sturm, one of the most dangerous members of the Conspiracy, at his fortress-like compound. A compound that had been guarded by constructs.

Augustine hadn't been there. His role had been different.

While they stormed Sturm's house, he was dismantling Sturm's allies. But he had watched a recording of that assault.

Augustine's memory served up the video of a monstrous mechanical horse with crocodile jaws charging at the camera, full speed, like a runaway train lit from within by a magical blue glow. Its mouth hung open, displaying two-foot-long steel teeth. A grenade hurtled toward it and exploded against the construct's chest, ripping a hole in the metal. Debris went flying. The construct stumbled, and then the jettisoned parts streamed back into it, reforming its body.

Sturm was a weather mage. Augustine had sunk hours and a lot of his resources into trying to tie Woodward to Sturm, and again, he'd failed. He knew Woodward was involved, he felt it with an intuition honed by years of experience. But he couldn't prove it.

Woodward had escaped all consequences of that investigation. He had always been a recluse, but since the Sturm affair, he practically vanished from the public eye. Yet here he was now, attacking the Harrisons.

"Why?" The word came out almost on its own, an extension of his thoughts.

Somehow, she understood him. "Kitty is an arcane creature born on Earth, one of a kind. He wants to take her apart. He wants to dissect her and use her body as a model for his next mechanical atrocity. He tried to buy Zeus years ago. We turned him down. He kept upping the price."

"How much did he offer?"

"Two-hundred and fifty million if Cornelius would keep Zeus calm and alive as long as possible during the vivisection."

Augustine recoiled.

Her eyes were terrible, frantic and brimming with pain. He hated it. He wanted to take that pain away from her, to reassure her, but he couldn't. Platitudes would only make things worse.

"Why Zeus? Woodward worked with the Conspiracy. He

had access to Harcourt, who had summoned Zeus. Why not just hire a summoner to get another specimen?"

"Because no summoner could keep a living animal calm while it was cut apart. And because Zeus was a bonded animal. No animal mage had been able to bond with a summon. Woodward thought that Zeus was unique. He wanted to study the bond and his body."

Revulsion cut through him, angry and cold.

"I should have known," she said, her voice defeated.

"How could you?"

They finally reached the townhouse parking lot. His phone vibrated. He glanced at it. Adrian Woodward owned three houses, one in California, one in Colorado, and this one, in Canyon Lake. He had boarded a private plane to Austin out of Denver International half an hour ago.

Augustine opened the file attachments. He found a series of images of Woodward's compound, a veritable fortress hiding behind a concrete wall. The house sat atop a hill overlooking a lake, with the nearest neighbor half a mile away.

"There is no time," she said, her voice hollow. "There's no time for backup. He will kill her tonight. She's still alive. I can still feel the bond with Celeste, a tiny sliver of it, and she would know if her cub had died. She would grieve and I would feel it, and if Kitty dies, I will lose them both."

The last traces of lust melted. He was back to his normal self, and he coldly calculated their options. None of them were good.

The legal system acknowledged its limitations when it came to Primes. When Houses came into conflict, they filed for official permission to engage in House warfare. Woodward hired someone to steal from House Harrison, and House Harrison's employees died as a result. They had more than enough for a Verona Exception, and with the right wording, he was certain their application for a feud would get approved, but that would take time. They didn't have any.

Storming the Woodward compound with MII without the proper permits was out of the question. It would expose his House and his company to sanctions and possible criminal liability. At a very basic level, it was illegal. And again, mobilizing an appropriate force would take time.

Their only option was a surgical strike. Right now, no money had exchanged hands. The only proof tying House Harrison and MII was sitting in his files, the contract Diana signed. He could delete it at any time. Only a handful of people knew where they were, and he trusted all of them. Even so, only he and Diana had the complete picture.

If they wanted to save the cub, they had to infiltrate the house. The best-case scenario had them sneaking in, finding the cub, and getting out. Undetected. The worst ended with all of them dead. From Denver, Woodward's flight to Austin would take roughly two hours, plus the drive to his mansion, because the tiny airport in Canyon Lake shut down at night. That would buy them another hour. Their chances were exponentially better with Woodward absent.

He made a decision. Really, it wasn't even a choice.

Diana turned to him, her face blank. Her tone was flat and clipped, the formality almost painful.

"Prime Montgomery, House Harrison thanks you for your assistance in this matter. You have more than honored the obligations of our agreement. I wish you success in your future endeavors. Should you ever need our assistance, House Harrison will stand by you."

He would have laughed, but she would have taken it badly. "Are you firing me?"

"Yes."

He waited.

She held out for another three seconds, but his silence broke her. "Woodward stole Kitty. I have evidence and the legal basis for a feud petition, but it will take too long. He will kill her tonight."

It was eerie how her thought patterns ran so parallel to his own.

"I'm going into that compound," she said. "You cannot come with me. If you do, your House and your firm will be implicated. We must part ways here."

"You need me," he said.

"I have seen his toys. They are nearly indestructible." The desperation in her voice cut at him. "I have to do this, but I probably won't survive it. I want you to live, Augustine. It's important to me."

He wanted to linger on that and figure out exactly what she meant, but now wasn't the right moment.

"You asked for my help. I will see it through."

"Your House…"

"My House isn't here, but I am. In my professional opinion, we have two choices: rescue or revenge. I prefer the rescue. We started this together, we will end this together."

"Augustine…"

He offered her a smile. "Let me make a quick call, and we'll be on our way."

***

The sky was a dusty purple, and the lake below stole its color, the water a dark mirror cradled by the rocky hills. The craggy crests and jagged, boulder-strewn cliffs looked nearly prehistoric. The only signs of civilization were an occasional outline of a roof and electric lights in the distance that left glowing trails on the water. And the pale monstrosity of a house sitting atop a neighboring hill.

Augustine peered through the scope of a sniper rifle. Canyon Lake was man-made and federally owned, managed by the U.S.

Army Corps of Engineers. The government had designated parts of the shoreline for public use. As luck would have it, one of these scenic overlooks gave them the perfect view of the Woodward estate. It spread slightly below them like an ancient fortress, poised behind an ornamental wall of Austin limestone that was topped with ornate wrought iron. The pure white house, if one could call a building of that size a house, rose three oversized stories up, beautifully illuminated by strategic, tinted lighting discreetly tucked away behind the landscape.

Augustine passed the rifle to Diana. She looked through the scope and frowned.

From the front, the house looked like any other ostentatious Texas mansion: huge lawn, vast stretches of paver-stone patios and walkways, trees vastly older than the buildings. A two-story arched gatehouse flanked by towers lorded over the main driveway.

The rear of the structure was like no other house—a solid block painted white. No doors, no windows. Just a cube of solid walls, three stories high and three hundred and fifty feet wide.

MII's intelligence on Woodward had been limited; however, they had a basic diagram of the house. Augustine's father had bought it from the builder for reasons unknown, and it had sat quietly in their internal files until Lina unearthed it and sent it to him.

Once again, his father's foresight had saved Augustine from the beyond. Eventually, Augustine would have to unpack the unpleasant cocktail of emotions that the realization brought up, but now wasn't the time.

Their target was to infiltrate the back of the house, that solid reinforced cube, which the builder had termed the Vault. The blueprint Lina had sent put the total square footage at a hundred twenty-two thousand, five hundred feet. It was the size of a Costco warehouse. Not only was the footprint staggering, but the costs of the land and construction had to have been astronomical. Even thirty years ago, when the compound had been built.

The Vault housed Woodward's laboratory: a warehouse of material storage, the crafting area where Woodward tinkered with his constructs, and, most importantly, a large indoor atrium labeled the "Menagerie," where he kept his animals.

Woodward collected rare species, specifically predators. The Menagerie served as a private zoo where they were housed until he decided to take them apart in an effort to understand how they worked. He seemed to be blissfully untroubled by the fact that none of the creatures survived the process.

In Woodward's view, there were three types of constructs: mechanical, magical, and biological. Animals and people fit into that last category, and the only difference between them and his creations were the materials from which they were made. That last bit came from a rare speech he'd given at an animator conference a decade ago. Animators were an odd lot, but even Woodward's words managed to disturb them enough to prevent any invitations since.

Augustine scrutinized the house one more time.

No guard house, no patrols, no floodlights. Nothing to indicate that a security force oversaw the mansion. Almost every House employed private protection. Hired guards were so common, their absence was both glaring and alarming.

That meant automated defenses. Woodward was likely to have turrets. Those two towers flanking the arched entrance were there for a reason, but Augustine wasn't worried about the turrets. They would be the least of their problems.

"Ten o'clock." Diana passed the rifle back to him.

Augustine looked through the scope, aiming in the direction she'd indicated.

There it was. A group of metal statues, arranged in a circle beneath the shadows of the trees, like some kind of art installation. Their odd contours threw him for a moment, until his brain made the connection.

Woodward's mansion was guarded by a pack of dinosaur constructs.

The constructs waited, motionless, arranged in three concentric circles. The outer ring consisted of the smallest creatures, six of them, roughly chest-high and resembling velociraptors. Not the actual versions from fossil records, which weighed about forty pounds, but the oversized movie versions, designed to terrify.

The second ring featured three thicker, larger creatures, odd hybrids of a triceratops and a prehistoric rhino.

The central beast towered above the rest, vaguely reminiscent of a T-Rex, poised on massive hind legs. Leaner than most museum reconstructions, the giant construct had longer forelimbs armed with sickle-shaped claws and a vicious, dragonlike head. Fourteen feet high and forty or so long, most of that length due to a tail constructed from squarish segments of razor-sharp blades.

The pseudo-T-Rex would lock on to the greatest threat, the triceratops herd would disable any vehicles, and the raptors would run down the individual intruders and mop up. All angles covered.

There was a towering arrogance in grouping them like that. Either Woodward didn't care, or he had liked the aesthetics of the arrangement. Like a small child, he'd set his toys up for display.

They truly looked like pieces of art, cohesive, elegant, slick, their lines efficient yet natural, as if they had evolved in some alternate reality and Woodward had reached into it and pulled them out.

"Just so we are on the same page," he murmured. "These are advanced guard models. Most constructs require an animator to activate them. These don't. Any movement will set them off.

They are equipped with visual, auditory, and infrared sensors, and they process their sensory input."

"Meaning?"

"I can fool their visual sensors, but my illusions have no substance. Unless the constructs register body heat and sound in addition to the visual feedback, they won't fall for my subterfuge. As you have seen yourself, they're difficult to destroy. They will reform, and magic will compensate for any damage, up to a point. However, they can be temporarily disabled with enough fire power. They will also re-form much more slowly than the constructs at Sturm's compound. That's the price of their autonomy."

She nodded.

"The only way to the Vault is from inside the house," he continued. "The walls are reinforced, and shooting blind at them is too risky."

Anything strong enough to breach the walls would almost certainly endanger the creatures inside.

"I'm reasonably sure the constructs won't enter the house," he said. "We have to make it to the front door and get in."

"What about the turrets?"

Ah. She spotted them as well. "I have a plan for the turrets. But I will require help with the constructs."

She narrowed her eyes. "What kind of help?"

"How fast are the wolves?"

"You want to use them as bait?"

"A distraction. We need something with body heat and a heartbeat to anchor the illusion. If they can buy us thirty seconds, they can disengage. The constructs will not leave the grounds. Woodward wouldn't want to open himself up to the liability of accidentally injuring civilians."

He felt a small pang of guilt. Before leaving MII, he had picked up the backpack he usually carried on covert missions. It waited in the backseat now, and inside it were five *bouncers*, small robotic gadgets designed specifically to mislead targeting sensors. The first set was a gift from Linus Duncan, but now MII bought them on a regular basis. They could use the *bouncers* to misdirect the constructs, but he didn't want to. He had a feeling they would need them, especially if things went to shit. And in his experience, things could always go to shit.

Diana frowned. "Sending the wolves against that many constructs means certain death."

"What if I reduce their numbers?"

"How?"

He turned back to the small parking lot where the Yukon waited. The rear hatch rose at his touch. He keyed the combination into the reinforced locker in the back. The top popped up half an inch. He grasped the panel, pulled it toward him until it slid free, set it aside, and retrieved a portable rocket launcher.

Diana looked at the collection of firearms, grenades, and ammo boxes inside the locker. Her mouth hung open.

For some reason, he felt ridiculously pleased with himself.

She turned and pointed at the contents of the locker.

He hid a grin and shrugged.

"Were you planning on taking over a small country?"

"I anticipated complications."

The shock in her eyes was so satisfying. He almost told her that MII had at least three of these vehicles, same loadout, same armor and run-flat tires, in every satellite office. Dallas, San Antonio, Austin, OKC, Amarillo, Los Angeles, Chicago, Atlanta… This one had come from Austin. Magic, no magic, Minor or Prime, bullets didn't care.

Instead, he kept his expression casual. "Would you like to pick something out? I can recommend a suitable firearm…"

She reached into the cargo area and pulled out a tactical short sword. She hefted the broad black blade and spun it in her hand like it weighed nothing.

Augustine smiled. She grinned back, and it was all teeth.

$$[\ 7 \ ]$$

The PGM-210, nicknamed the Lance, was a step-up from the FGM-148 Javelin. The pinnacle of portable "fire-and-forget" anti-tank weaponry, it spat out guided Archangel missiles—tandem-charge warheads with official ranges of two point eight kilometers. In practice, a skilled user could take out targets up to four kilometers away.

It was only eight hundred meters between them and the target below. Augustine planted himself, sitting cross-legged in the dirt, the Lance resting on his shoulder.

"3...2...1..."

Diana had asked him to give her a count. The wolves didn't react well to sudden loud noises.

"Fire."

He squeezed the trigger.

The Lance spat the warhead with a crack. The small missile rocketed toward the compound, its fire trail lighting up the night. The little artificial star fell in the middle of the construct huddle and exploded.

BOOM!

A plume of dark smoke erupted.

The tops of the towers split, and twin turrets rose up, turning.

"Fire."

He squeezed the trigger. The left turret vanished in an explosion of fire and smoke.

"Fire."

The right turret disintegrated.

He set the Lance to the side and rolled to his feet, sweeping it back up. Sliding it into the locker and jumping into the Yukon's passenger seat took barely a second. Diana took off, the Yukon speeding down the mountain road, its lights off.

Behind them, a high-voltage searchlight swept the hillside. Woodward's automated systems searching for them.

Diana took a turn at hair-raising speed. He was almost sure the SUV's tires left the ground. The road was pitch-black. He couldn't see shit. Augustine gripped the handle on the door.

The SUV rolled over something.

"Lights," he squeezed out.

"No need. Trust me."

The Yukon went airborne and landed with a clang. He saw Woodward's estate looming in front of them, the two mangled turrets smoking on top of the towers.

Diana stood on the gas. The Yukon surged forward like a runaway battering ram.

The metal gate flashed before them. He didn't even have a chance to brace for impact.

The SUV plowed into the gate. Metal screeched, and then they were through, speeding down the driveway.

A massive shape charged at them through the trees—a triceratops construct, illuminated by eerie blue magic from within.

Ahead, stainless-steel pillars emerged from the pavement, rising. Defensive bollards blocking access to the house.

Diana threw the wheel to the left.

The car turned, sliding into a skid. For a terrifying moment, they hurtled sideways, straight at the bollard barrier, so fast that his life had no chance to flash before his eyes.

The SUV screeched to a halt two feet from the pillars.

Diana shoved her door open. He jumped out from his side, carrying a duffel in his left hand and a cluster of Helios flash bombs in his right. They ran between the bollards and dashed to the front door. Behind them a tortured metal groan announced a construct smashing into the Yukon.

Augustine spun around. The pack of velociraptors was charging toward them at full speed, four of them, the magic powering them blazing brighter. Behind them, the mangled T-Rex struggled forward, dragging itself across the ground as pieces of its body slowly floated back toward it.

Augustine pulled the pins from the flash bombs, hurled them at the SUV, and sprinted to the door. Diana flew ahead of him.

The night turned white, illuminating the stairs, the double doors, and the armored shutters descending over the windows. The Helios explosions would burn for three seconds, their intense bursts of light designed to damage retinas and image sensors.

One. He snapped his magic like a whip, anchoring it to the two lupine shapes running back, toward the mangled front gate turning the wolves into Diana and his doppelgangers.

Two. He wrapped his power around himself and Diana, willing them to melt into the night.

Three. He bounded up the stairs to the front doors, pulling at the zipper on the duffel. Diana was already there.

Augustine chanced a quick glance over his shoulder. Two of the velociraptors had veered back, chasing after illusions of their doppelgangers. The triceratops had followed. The T-Rex was halfway up, and the two remaining velociraptors were sixty feet away.

He pulled his Angstadt Arms MDP-9 out, unfolding the stock in a fluid motion, and thrust it at her.

Diana ignored it. "The door, Augustine."

He extracted the party crasher strip from the duffel, peeled the breacher tape off, and stuck it to the door.

The first construct leaped at Diana. She stepped out of the way and hacked at it with her tactical blade.

Augustine slid the detonator into the strip.

Diana became a whirlwind of controlled savagery. Pieces from the two constructs rained onto the ground.

He spun around, lunged at her, and knocked her off the stairs to the side. They landed on the pavers, and he pressed the remote firing switch.

Another explosion tore through the night.

Augustine rolled to his feet. The T-Rex bore down on them, twenty feet away and closing. Diana leaped to the top of the stairs. Augustine sprinted after her. They shot through the smoking doorway just as the T-Rex's metal teeth scissored the air behind them.

Augustine slid across the polished marble of the foyer and spun around. The constructs halted at the doorstep, motionless.

Diana inhaled, sampling the air like one of her wolves. Her eyes glowed, and she raised her sword and ran to the left down the hallway.

God fucking damnit! There she goes again.

He shouldered his weapon and followed.

THE SCENT BURNED LIKE A RED-HOT WIRE GLOWING AND dragging her through the cavernous house. Kitty, mixed with the odor of a human. All of her senses went into overdrive. Nothing existed except the cub and the scumbag who touched her.

A door loomed, blocking her way. She pounded a kick into the wood. It held.

Another.

One more.

Again.

A strong hand grabbed her by the shoulder and she snapped, nearly biting Augustine's fingers.

"Wrong spot," he said.

He stepped in front of her, gently pushing her to the side, and leaned back. His foot shot out like a hammer and smashed into the door near the lock. The wood splintered, and he casually kicked the door again, knocking it open.

She pushed past him and dashed into the room. A man stood in the small bedroom, his hands raised. She inhaled, drawing the scents in, and snarled in pure frustration.

Not here.

"Just a vet," the man said quietly, pronouncing each word carefully. He held himself like he was facing a rabid dog.

A vet? No. A shitstain, an accessory to torture and vivisection, murderer...

"I am just a vet. A doctor. I take care of them..."

She leaped onto him. Her fingers locked around his throat, and she dragged him closer until a mere inch of space separated their faces.

"Where is my cub?"

Sweat drenched his hairline. He went pale, his pupils widening into black pools filled with terror. Fear dripped from him, sticky and viscous.

"She asked you a question." Augustine's voice was sharpened ice.

"In the Vault, they're all in the Vault," the man croaked.

She dragged him into the hallway by his neck. "Show me!"

The man pointed down the hallway.

"Walk," she snarled into his ear.

They started down the hallway, walking in step, her hand still locked around his windpipe from the side. One squeeze. That's all it would take. One delicious, satisfying squeeze.

They hurried through the house, passing doors and hallways, to the back, behind the kitchen where a solid wall bisected the building in half. A metal door with a numerical lock waited in the center.

She hurled him at it. "Open it."

His shoulder struck the wall. He yelped and turned to Augustine, his eyes shivering with desperation. "If I open it, will you let me go?"

She hissed at him.

Augustine's hand gently rested on her shoulder. "Priorities. Kitty is all that matters. He can open the door."

The human part of her, the calmer rational part that realized when she was three years old that she was not a panther but a person, slid into the driver's seat.

"Fine. I give my word."

The man keyed a code into the lock with trembling fingers. Metal clanged, something whirred, and the door slid aside.

Augustine pointed his gun at the man. "Run."

The man turned and sprinted through the house, his feet thudding on the floor. He would not be back. She had seen enough people in blind panic, and that man was running for his life.

She dove through the hole where the door used to be. A warehouse spread before her—concrete floor, concrete walls, shelves filled with lumber and metal, and directly in front of them, a hundred feet away, another doorway filled with electric light.

She almost sprinted to it, but Augustine caught her hand in his. The sudden warmth of his touch was like a burn to her overclocked senses.

"Together," he said, and it sounded like a plea.

She forced herself to slow to his pace. They ran across the warehouse to the door. He paused before it, checking, his gun raised, and stepped through. She followed.

A rectangular room, a hundred and fifty feet long and three hundred feet wide. Kennels lining the walls. A yellow line painted three feet from the bars with the word *SAFE* stenciled on the outside of it. And eyes, looking at her from the cages with silent desperation.

A kaleidoscope of scents swirled around her: bear, tiger, fox... So many, so many sparks of life reaching out for connection, some strong, some fading, all terrified. Her magic splayed out, and she felt them all at once. If they had voices that could speak, they would be screaming, "Free us!"

She was lost. Overwhelmed by the intensity of it all. By the suffering, by the hopelessness. They didn't comprehend, they only knew they were trapped and they were scared, but the human part of her understood what they could not—why they were here, what would happen to them, and how much it would hurt.

She tried to breathe, but there was a steel band around her chest, and it couldn't expand. A solid clump blocked her throat. Tears blurred her vision, and the world faded into a haze of red that cut like broken glass. A dark chasm opened by her feet, and she teetered on the precipice. If she fell, she would come apart, unravel like a tattered cloth, melting into the two dozen animals scrambling for her magic.

She heard something, a voice, words, but she couldn't make them out. Something wrapped around her, solid, protective, pulling her back from the bottomless pit of pain.

"Diana, come back to me. I need you here with me."

Augustine.

She locked her hands on his arms, still blind, and held on until she could breathe again. His scent washed over her, a barrier to all others, and she locked onto it and took a small step back from the edge.

Gradually, with agonizing slowness, her inner world reasserted its balance. Her mental defenses rose, shielding her from the sparks scraping at her with their claws, begging for connection and safety.

A slow breath.

Another.

She had almost lost herself. It was the fate feared by every animal mage. She had come this close only once before, when she had been young and inexperienced. She was no longer an unsure 13-year-old, she knew the risks, and she ought to have made preparations.

It was Kitty, the timer on her phone warning her that too much time passed since the cub last fed, Celeste's suffering, Kayson's and Aleah's loved ones' grief, and Woodward's imminent return. They had all combined inside a pressure cooker, and it nearly broke her.

And then there was Augustine, both making it all worse and infinitely better. If it weren't for him, when Woodward did return, he would find her on the floor, catatonic, a living husk without will or reason.

"Diana…" Augustine's whisper was like a velvet caress.

She squeezed his arms tighter around herself, savoring his touch for the last time, and then pushed free.

"I'm fine. Thank you."

She didn't look at his face. She didn't know what she would see. Concern? Revulsion? Pity? She couldn't risk it. Not now.

The scents still clamored for her attention, but she sorted through them with confident ease.

There it was, the familiar warm scent, like a dandelion made of sunshine. The moment her consciousness brushed it, a surge of magic focused on her, insistent, demanding a connection. She forced herself to rebuff it, walked toward the cage on the far left, and stopped before the bars.

Kitty pawed at the bars with her fuzzy, blue murder mittens. "Meeya!"

It wasn't even a meow. It was a demand that said, "Well? Aren't you going to get me out? What took you so long?"

A padlock secured the door. She almost panicked for a split second, and then Augustine reached over and unlocked it. She blinked at the keys in his hands.

"It was hanging by the doorway," he said. "They're numbered."

She swung the door open and scooped the cub into her arms. The tiny blue tiger licked her face. They were not bonded, but the cub sensed the magic that connected her and Celeste. She knew that she was with her other mother.

Augustine spun around and fired. A stream of bullets tore through the Menagerie and bit into a construct by the doorway, a large feline shape crafted with metal and magic. Strangely shaped parts rained onto the floor. The construct sank. Blue magic pulsed, and the scattered parts flew back to it, sliding seamlessly into place.

A second construct stalked through the doorway and paused next to the first, its lines sleek.

Panthers. He dared.

The beginning of a growl rumbled in her throat, and she hid it. Some people might have found the metal cats beautiful. But she saw them for what they were—tortured imitations of the original, striving to capture the grace and lethal force of the true creature and hopelessly failing.

A dark-haired man stepped through the doorway. He was of average height, with an unremarkable build and a forgettable face, just another man in his early fifties. He had a narrow face, a prominent nose, and dark eyes under low, thick eyebrows. He smelled odd, like a tree scorched by lightning, the hints of familiar human sweat and skin oils mixing with the sharp tinge of ozone.

She had met him only twice, but his face and his scent were branded into her memory, because she had realized that he was a threat the moment he tried to buy Zeus.

"Trespassing. Vandalism."

His voice had an odd echo as if he were speaking into a hidden microphone. It filled the space around them, and the hairs on the back of her arms rose in response.

"Destruction of property. Breaking and entering, or is it burglary?"

Woodward's tone sounded calm and methodical, devoid of emotion, but the echoes of his words bounced around her like rocks tossed onto hard concrete. That eerie sound combined with his scent tripped some sort of alarm deep within her. She knew with complete certainty that Death was here and he was staring into her eyes.

"I had expected such foolishness from Prime Harrison. Her magic clouds her judgement, and her thought patterns are primitive and short-sighted. Much like the other creatures here, she doesn't understand consequences. But you, Prime Montgomery, are a man of logic and reason. You should have realized how futile this venture would be. It couldn't have been money. Was it hubris? Or was it the promise of sex? I really must know."

<hr>

THE METAL PANTHER HAD FINISHED REASSEMBLING ITSELF. Talons the size of steak knives, razor-sharp metal teeth, and advanced response protocols. Augustine lowered his gun. He had been aiming at Woodward. The construct had thrust itself into the path of the bullets, but not before the first few had hit Woodward.

The man had blocked them with his arm.

There was no blood. No obvious shield. No telltale thickening of magic signifying the presence of an aegis, a shielder mage.

How? He had shot enough bullets to amputate his arm at the elbow. A shiver of worry squirmed through Augustine. This was outside the expected parameters of Woodward's power.

He forced himself to concentrate on the immediate. The known. Two constructs, clearly slaughter class, designed to rapidly murder anything in their way. One animator. Augustine scrutinized the doorway, but nothing else came through.

Woodward himself appeared less of a threat at first glance—lean, wearing black trousers and a thick black turtleneck that had become the uniform for aging tech entrepreneurs. But there was something odd in the way he moved. A heaviness to his steps… He was standing still now, and still, he held himself in an unnatural way. It wasn't readily apparent. Augustine had to focus, and even then, it kept eluding him.

Time was short. He had seconds to figure this out.

Looking for the source of the wrongness, Augustine replayed Woodward's entrance in his head, the way he emerged step by step through the doorway.

There.

A human body was a collection of unified parts, bone connected by cartilage and powered by muscle. He'd spent a lot of time studying human bodies. He knew how they moved, how they were put together, and how to break and tear them apart. There were several muscles that connected the legs to the rest of the body and enabled bipedal motion. When humans walked, these muscles tugged on the torso, causing a slight turn. If you attached a light to a person's breastbone, the light would shift side to side with each step. It was a minute movement, but crucial to evaluating one's gait.

Woodward's torso didn't shift. It remained perfectly straight, as if set atop his legs yet still separate from them. And now he stood with unnatural stillness. Even disciplined, focused soldiers locked into the position of attention couldn't stay perfectly still. The human body constantly made minor adjustments to balance. Human chests rose and fell. Blood pulsed through veins, and muscles contracted and twitched.

The implications sank in. Alarm struck him in a flash, as if someone injected ice straight into his bones, and then he was calm. Fear, anger, and doubt vanished. He dropped into a familiar empty space, where only he and the target existed.

In a prolonged fight, Woodward would have the advantage. He wouldn't get tired. This would have to be done fast. And it would take everything he had. There would be no do-overs.

Every mage saw their magic differently. For Augustine, it was a translucent flame. A nearly invisible fire that coated his form, constrained by his will into a uniform sheath and constantly fueled by his body. If he didn't bleed some of it off by maintaining a constant illusion, it would grow too dense and break its cage. When he activated his field, that phantom fire swelled, and he punched the ground with it, detonating his power like a grenade, with illusions sprouting in the wake of the blast.

But right now, he gathered it all and sent it inward, a torrent of ghostly flames swirling into his chest, through his body, and down his back, into the seal branded there.

The scars ignited.

Agony.

Familiar. Welcome. The price he paid. It hurt the same every time, never less than the first moment the brand had sizzled as the white-hot wires burned their way into his flesh.

Woodward's words skimmed the surface of Augustine's awareness. He was insulting Diana, an obvious baiting tactic. Augustine glanced at her. Her eyes glowed with magic, brimming with power so bright, the entirety of her irises and sclera were pools of gold. Somehow he saw understanding in that radiance. They didn't need to talk. They were perfectly in sync.

His back was a pit of pain, so intense his vision wavered. He called up the complex lines of the Phantom House spell in his mind, channeling the magic through the seal in a specific pattern to recreate it.

Diana stepped forward. That same otherworldly predatory grace he saw on the hill suffused her movements. Her voice was low and steady. She spoke with the absolute authority of a Prime.

"You think you've improved on nature with your imitations."

"I know I have." Woodward's voice rang with arrogance.

She swung her sword, and there was something shockingly feline in the movement. It was as if she'd shed her human skin and become a predatory cat without shifting a single muscle.

He'd pumped so much power into the seal, he no longer felt his body, just a swirling mass of magic and pain. In a moment, it would break past his control and erupt. His fingers squeezed the metal spheres of the *bouncers* in his pocket.

One more breath. Hold.

"Today I will teach you the difference," the human panther promised.

The constructs lunged forward in unison. She had given him a clear shot at Woodward.

Augustine hurled the *bouncers* into the space between them and Woodward. The walnut-sized spheres bounced and exploded in fans and pulses of sound, light, and heat, spinning and rolling in random directions.

Woodward flinched, clamping a hand over his left eye.

Augustine grasped the scalding current of magic emanating from the seal on his back and slammed it into the chaos of heat and light. In an instant, he was a shadow, a faceless dark phantom in the shape of his body. Pools of darkness spawned across the floor, birthing shadowy doppelgangers, one after another, all charging in random directions.

Augustine sprinted left, reached again for the searing magic still streaming from the seal, and pulled it around himself. It sank into his skin.

He vanished.

"How thrilling!" Woodward screamed into the cacophony. "I feel honored. You showed me your power. I will show you mine!"

Augustine was almost to him.

"See what all of this was for. Witness it. Understand it, and despair!"

Woodward ripped off his clothes. They came free like they were tissue paper. His legs, the left half of his torso all the way to the collarbone, and his arms were an amalgam of metal and high-performance plastic, woven together with sick artistry and bright blue magic. His right half was still mostly human but protected by ornate skin-tight armor. Long scars cleaved Woodward's neck.

It was exactly as Augustine feared. The moment Woodward walked in, the wrongness of his posture, the oddness of his stance, combined with his obsession with animals and bodies, all pointed to this conclusion. Woodward had found a way to fuse a construct to himself.

It shouldn't have been possible. And yet here it was.

The phantoms flittered around Woodward. One of them punched him, and Woodward staggered back. Shock slapped his face.

Iillusions had no substance. It was a known fact. But these were not regular illusions. They were House Montgomery phantoms. That punch was a concentrated knot of Augustine's power, and Woodward's human brain and senses recognized it as a threat.

Woodward's construct limbs split, releasing seven-inch-long

daggers. He sliced at the incoming phantoms in a frenzy. The clinical part of Augustine warned him that Woodward was faster and stronger.

Time slowed, the seconds crawling by, as Augustine closed the distance between him and the animator. No opening. No target for a knife. But Woodward still needed an intact brain and a functioning spinal cord.

He was almost to Woodward now. The air smelled of blood. He caught a glimpse of Diana tearing at the constructs. Somehow she had managed to shred both of them with her ferocity, her frenzied strikes keeping both panthers in states of partial collapse. Any other time, the beauty of her violence would have been incredibly erotic; however, he saw only blood. It saturated her torn clothes. She flung it to the floor with every strike. Constructs didn't bleed.

Sometimes victory required sacrifice.

In front of him, Woodward swung wide, slicing a phantom in half. For a fraction of a breath, the animator's arms were open, his chest exposed.

Augustine slipped forward, all of his martial arts training condensed into this short, fluid movement.

Woodward saw him and stabbed with his right arm, trying to skewer him through the stomach. Augustine twisted out of the way. Pain sliced his abdomen on the left side— Woodward's blade grazing him. He'd known he wouldn't be able to avoid the stab completely, but it didn't matter. He had moved into position.

Augustine hugged Woodward, chest to chest, locked his left hand around the top of Woodward's head, grasped the man's chin with his right, and twisted up.

His neck snapped with a dry crunch.

Augustine let go and stepped back.

Woodward's body teetered. The brilliant blue magic animating it vanished like a snuffed-out candle. For a moment the form held before the body fell apart, scattering onto the floor like a bucket of loose LEGO pieces.

Behind him twin thuds announced the deaths of the metal panthers.

Augustine drew in a ragged breath. The magic drain hit him like a runaway semi. His legs folded, and then he was looking up at the ceiling.

Something clanged. He craned his neck just in time to see the massive metal door thud into place, sealing the exit.

[8]

Diana sliced through Augustine's shirt. It came apart, and she pulled it all the way open. A narrow horizontal slash gaped across his abdomen. Woodward's knife had cut through the muscles of his stomach. She could see the angry bulge of intestines soaked in blood.

Panic whipped her. She took off, limping toward a small room in the corner, partitioned off from the rest of the Menagerie by temporary office walls and a flimsy door.

She knew she was bleeding, but she didn't care.

She rammed the door with her shoulder. It burst open, revealing a small room with a refrigerator, food dishes in the sink, a stack of white towels. She grabbed one of the latter. Her nose caught a hint of bleach. Clean. She shoved the towel under the faucet, wet it, and raced back.

He was exactly where she'd left him. She dropped next to him and plastered the wet towel over the wound.

"Diana…" he said.

"Your stomach is lacerated," she told him. "If we don't keep it wet, your intestines will dry out."

Red spread through the towel, and she almost cried.

"You're bleeding," he said.

She tapped the towel in place, trying to push it tighter against the wound without hurting him.

"You have a deep stab wound on your thigh. You need a tourniquet or you'll bleed out."

She ignored him.

"Diana!"

"Not yet!" She couldn't walk with a tourniquet.

Diana took off again, making a frantic circle around the Menagerie. A few minutes later she landed next to him again, this time with a canvas sack, a pair of scissors, and an oversized metal spoon. Augustine was right. The wound was deep, and the stream of blood was too fast. It would soak though a makeshift bandage. She had to cut off the flow.

He watched her cut the sack into five-inch strips and fold them into one thick, long bandage. She stripped her pants off. The deep hole in her leg gaped like a red mouth. Blood ran down her skin.

She looped the improvised dressing above the wound and tied it into a half knot in a flash of pain. The spoon was next; she placed it on top of the knot and tied the strips again.

"Let me." He pushed himself half-upright.

"I'm fine."

He gripped the spoon and rotated it, winding it like a clock. Pain squeezed her leg. Diana cried out.

Another turn. Another. The flow of blood stopped. Augustine looped the tails of the dressing over the spoon, tied it in place, and collapsed.

She lay flat on her back. The adrenaline had worn off, and she had nothing left. Kitty, who'd been trailing behind her during her frantic search, padded over, sniffed at her blood, and flopped on the floor between them.

"Any way out?" Augustine asked.

Diana wanted to lie to him but couldn't. "No. There is no way to open the door, and there is no cell service."

"That's to be expected." His voice was quiet. "We're in a bunker with four-foot-thick concrete walls."

Woodward's death must've triggered some sort of failsafe, because the steel door blocking their exit had no lock. She couldn't find any mechanism to open it. It was just a wall of metal sealing them in. There were no windows, no exits. Nothing in the Menagerie could breach the reinforced concrete walls. She'd hoped for a landline in the little room where she found the towels, but there had been none.

They were truly trapped.

If they didn't get to a hospital in the next hour or two, Augustine would die. She didn't know if his intestines were perforated. Even if they weren't, they would dry out. He could go into sepsis, and he was still bleeding.

If she didn't get medical treatment soon, she would lose her leg, and then she would die.

She could almost hear Woodward laughing. They would all die here. Together. Eventually someone would open that door and find three human corpses.

She forced herself to reach for the pocket in her jacket, pulled out a pouch filled with liquid, unscrewed the lid, revealing a rubber nipple, and offered it to Kitty. The cub sucked on the pouch, making greedy growling noises.

Diana waited until all of Celeste's milk was gone, typed a message on her phone, removed the password, and put it down next to her.

"What does it say?" he asked.

"It says House Harrison will give five million to whoever brings Kitty back to my House alive. She just had her milk. That gives her a couple of days. I left a dish of water on the floor.

"It will be fine," he told her. "We will be okay."

It would not be okay. There was no escape.

"Stay with me, Diana?" he asked.

She turned to him and forced a smile.

His eyes weren't wholly green. They were a light, beautiful hazel, a ring of greyish green with a starburst of golden brown around the pupil.

It hit her. His magic was gone. Augustine was spent. She was seeing the real him, and she looked at him, really *looked* at him.

His shoulders were broader. She'd caught a glimpse of his true body during the fight with the Hesters, but now the hard muscle cording his frame was obvious. An old scar sliced through his left cheek, cleaving his upper lip in the corner. Stubble roughened his jaw. His features had lost their flawless perfection, but somehow that only heightened their impact. She'd always assumed he had reshaped his face with his illusions. She was wrong. Augustine still looked like himself. Her deadly prince was truly that beautiful.

She sat up, pulled off her jacket, rolled it into a wad, and gently tilted him up to slide it under his head.

A massive scar scoured his back. She gasped. An arcane circle, not just drawn but burned into his skin, so deep the lines of the sigil were shallow trenches in his flesh.

"Who did this to you?"

"I did it to myself."

She slid the jacket under his head and lowered him. "Why?"

"I was weak. I needed power."

Sometimes magic users drew sigils on themselves to boost their magic. Very rarely, they tattooed themselves, a process that was inherently dangerous. Arcane circles and sigils required incredible precision. A tiny mistake could cause one to lose their magic and even their life. She had seen statistics somewhere, and the survival rate of those who resorted to tattoos was tiny, less than one percent.

This wasn't a tattoo. This was so much worse, a seal permanently burned into his flesh. There were no statistics for this because nobody would be foolish enough to try it.

She slid next to Augustine, so close they were almost touching. Kitty padded closer. Diana felt the familiar insistent push of the cub's magic. Like a persistent kitten booping her hand with her head, demanding a pet. Kitty was looking for a bond. As always, Diana forced herself to ignore it. The cub tried again, then gave up, and tucked herself into the crook of Diana's body. She wrapped her arm around Kitty.

She had failed her and Celeste. Thinking about it would only unravel her further, and she didn't want that. She wanted to spend these last minutes with Augustine.

"Tell me about the circle," she whispered.

"My father and I never got along. He thought I was irresponsible and naïve, and I thought he was rigid and controlling. A man without dreams, who settled for mundane drudgery and kept trying to drag me down with him. I wanted to be free. I had plans. I wanted to be a spy. Someone who kept my country safe."

"You would've made an exceptional spy," she told him.

"I would have. When I was in my early twenties, my family was attacked," Augustine said. "They were well prepared. I found my mother, Verena, and my brother bleeding out on the floor, next to three corpses. My other sister, Seraphina, my aunt, and my father did not survive. We couldn't afford to look weak. If it became known that the attack had succeeded, our enemies would rip us apart. Half of my family was dead. I had to keep my mother and my remaining siblings safe. So, I became my father. I cloaked myself in illusion, put on his face, and went to work the next day."

How horrifying.

"For two years I was both him and me, pretending to lead MII, giving myself orders and carrying them out, trying to keep the ship that was our House and our firm afloat in the storm.

Except that Primes can see through each other's illusions. For the deception to succeed, I had to be stronger than any other illusion Prime. I needed the kind of power nobody could match."

"Did it hurt?"

"It did. It still does every time I use it."

"You lied to me," she told him.

"When?"

"You told me your illusions weren't corporeal, but I saw them hurt Woodward."

He sighed. "That was a House spell. The seal makes it possible for me to access them without needing to draw a circle. It is called Doppelganger. When I create phantoms, I can infuse them with my magic. Each of them was a supercharged mani-festation of my power, so when they came into contact with Woodward, his magic recognized them as a genuine threat. They hurt him, but they can't actually injure him. So you see, it wasn't a complete lie."

"Just a partial one?"

"Yes." Augustine was looking at her, and his eyes were so warm. "Why is it I tell you all my secrets?"

"Because you like the way I look draped over a tree branch?"

He tried to laugh, coughed instead, and grimaced.

She reached over and caressed his face. She was so bold now, because it didn't matter. They were dying.

"How did you know it was me?" he asked softly. "When you saw me on the street this morning?"

"I always recognize you."

"How?"

She shrugged, ignoring a slash of pain from her wounds. "I just know. You are the one. My special one."

"Why me?"

"I don't know."

"What is it about me you like?" He sounded so puzzled.

"Everything. The way you think, the way you fight, the way you look at me. I like your scent. I like your eyes." She leaned forward and brushed a kiss on his lips. "I like the strength of your arms, and how it feels when you touch me. I knew the moment we met."

"Why didn't you tell me?"

"Because you are who you are, and I am who I am. You shouldn't have come with me, Augustine. I wish you hadn't. I wish you were outside. I wish both of us were outside, with Kitty."

He reached over and took her hand. His fingers were so warm.

"How can you do this?" he asked.

"Which part?"

"Running up the hill. Killing constructs. Lifting me just now."

She squeezed his hand. "Have you ever wondered why animals are so much stronger than us? Yes, we can talk about differences in muscle fibers and compare the number of motor neurons, but at our cores we are powered by the same biological mechanisms. And yet a bobcat who is a fraction of our size can leap twelve feet and bring down an adult deer with a single bite. Why is it we are so weak, pound for pound?"

"I don't know," he said. "Because we don't have to be strong?"

"Yes. We have forgotten how to be animals. We have guns, knives, clothes… Magic. But animal mages are different. We remember how because we bond with animals from birth."

She kissed his knuckles and smiled.

"Animal mages plan very carefully for their children, because our first bond defines our personality and character. I was the oldest of my siblings, and my magic marked me as a Prime when I was born. I would be the head of the House, so my parents chose a panther. Not a leopard. A black jaguar. For the first three years of my life, I thought I was a panther.

Weaker than my panther family but so much stronger than a human."

She had never talked about this, but for some reason it felt right to tell him. She was beginning to feel the first feathery touches of dizziness.

"My brother was the second-born. My parents counted on him to support me. They wanted him to understand the importance of family and loyalty. He was bonded to a wolf. He took to it too well. He is a wolf in all but skin. Patient, cunning, and pessimistic. I don't see him often, but if I ever called for help, he would come.

"Cornelius was supposed to bond with a bear. But he made his own choice. Instead of making a pact with the Kodiak my parents prepared for him, he formed his first bond with a fat, silly raccoon who got stuck in the chimney of the fireplace. People think raccoons are aggressive, but they are shy and timid."

"Your parents didn't like that, did they?" he asked.

"No. My mother decided that Cornelius was a failure. She called him a critter and wrote him off. While Blake and I learned to fight, Cornelius treated injured squirrels and sang little lullabies to abandoned kittens. I love my youngest brother so much. My childhood was grim. My parents were cold."

"Why do you think that is?"

She sighed. "Because we learn early on that it hurts when the creatures around us die. For me, there is no difference between a bird I fed for the past couple of months and a human who worked for me for ten years. It all hurts the same. And when your children or your parents die, it hurts most of all. That's why so many of us kill ourselves. My parents were shielding themselves and tried to teach us to do the same. It was meant to keep us safe."

"But you are not like that," he said.

"No. And neither is Blake. We had Cornelius. He didn't

know how to be cold. When we were children, I would go to him in my darkest moments, and he was always sweet and kind. Being near him made me feel better. Made me feel loved. I treasured it. Then one day Cornelius stopped talking to me. We grew apart and lost touch. Later I found out that my mother had bound him to Adam Pierce, and Adam tormented him. So I confronted my mother, and that is why I'm now the head of my House."

"Did you kill her?" he asked.

"No. She and my father retired. I think it was a relief to her. She never dealt well with the pressure. I don't hate her, Augustine. I understand her reasons, but I reject them. When I took over, I promised myself that I would never make the same choices she made. I like to think I was a better head of the House. More human. I suppose Blake will take over now."

He squeezed her hand.

"I have no regrets," she whispered. "It was a good life. And I got to hold your hand at the end."

The wall across from them exploded.

Diana jerked upright.

A small figure stumbled through the hole, slid across the floor, carried forward by her own momentum, careened off-balance, then straightened herself.

Was she hallucinating?

The figure pulled back the hood of her sweatshirt, revealing blond hair pulled back into a ponytail and blue eyes on a delicate face.

"Hi!" Arabella announced.

Augustine sat up, wincing. "Our ride is here."

Diana pivoted to him.

He smiled at her.

"How?" she squeezed out.

"He called me two hours ago," Arabella told her, walking over. "He said to extract the two of you if he didn't text or call by eight. This is me extracting." She shook out her right hand and rubbed her knuckles.

How? How did she get through the wall? She hadn't transformed. Had she *punched* it?

The youngest Baylor took in the blood, bandages, and the red-stained towel on Augustine's stomach. "I have medical on standby. They are ten minutes down the road for plausible deniability. Also, Bern is wiping Woodward's servers as we speak. Before you say anything, we will forward you a copy of the data dump. Discreetly, of course. Did I do good?"

"You did well," Augustine said. He didn't seem the least bit surprised.

The fractured picture came together in Diana's head. He hadn't wanted to involve MII, and she hadn't wanted to involve her House because of legal liabilities. If either of them had mobilized their forces, it would've been noticed, and once the aftermath of their assault on the compound was discovered, questions would follow.

If the Baylors or Rogans mobilized their forces, someone would have noted that as well, but nobody would even think to connect a single young woman to a massive hole in Woodward's compound. Arabella Baylor was a neutral third party. She kept a very low profile. Her short absence from the Baylors' compound would be easy to explain away. Once her cousin destroyed the surveillance data, nobody would ever know how Woodward died.

Augustine knew, Diana realized. He knew the whole time that a rescue was coming, and he let her think they were dying. She had told him everything. For a moment she wasn't sure if she was relieved or mortified.

"We're all good!" Arabella called.

A second figure in a hoodie marched through the hole, this person slightly taller and more broadly built. She pulled her hood back, looked around, taking in the rows of cages. She put her hands on her hips and frowned. "This is one fucked-up zoo."

"Is that who I think it is?" Augustine asked.

"This is Tia Madero," Arabella said. "I thought I might need backup. Oh my God, what is that? Is that Zeus' baby?"

"What is your plan for the blood and DNA?" Augustine said.

"The biological cleanup crew." Arabella pointed to the cages with the animals. "They are very good at destroying blood. I brought a specialist to help."

A third person ran through the hole, a child with dark hair and a worried look on her face.

"Matilda," Diana breathed. "No…"

Her niece saw her. Matilda's brown eyes widened. "Aunt Diana!"

Kitty turned, her eyes fixed on Matilda.

Diana saw her niece stop in mid-step. A thin ribbon of magic brushed over Diana's senses. She tried to shout a warning, but it was too late. The two children saw each other, and she was powerless to stop it.

Matilda opened her mouth. A beautiful soft song spilled out, a wordless note that soared like a bright hymn fighting against the brutal cruelty of the bunker. The tigrionex cub snarled, echoing it. An eerie purple light shivered around Kitty's neck, the beginnings of tentacle tendrils, still too short to be noticed with the naked eye, glowing with arcane radiance.

The song faded, and Matilda's voice came forth, otherworldly and suffused with power.

"The pact is made."

The hospital bed was surprisingly comfortable, Augustine reflected. But then, considering the amount of money he spent on MII's infirmary, that was to be expected.

Arabella had borrowed Connor's medics. In less than an hour, both he and Diana were patched up and on their way to Houston via a MII helicopter. They didn't speak during the trip. He had misled Diana, and she was angry. He could almost feel the intensity of her indignation radiating outward like heat. Once they landed, her people picked her up, while his people took him to the infirmary, and they parted ways without a single word.

The infirmary was on the twenty-second floor, and from his bed he could see Houston, a multitude of electric lights glowing like coals scattered across dark ashes. They must've given him a strong cocktail, because he wasn't given to poetic nonsense.

A careful knock sounded through the room. He glanced at the doorway and saw Arabella rapping her knuckles on the doorframe. Augustine nodded.

She walked in and set a high-capacity storage drive on the side table. Woodward's dirty secrets.

"All the animals have been evacuated," she reported.

"Blake Harrison?"

She nodded. "He just appeared out of nowhere with a pack of wolves and three horse trailers."

"What's your opinion of him?"

She frowned. "Unsettling. I've met him before, and he is very good at pretending to be human. Tonight, he didn't bother."

His original assessment proved correct. House Harrison was full of interesting surprises.

"About that recommendation," she said.

"Are you sure it's what you want?" he asked. "It will be a lot of work."

Her expression became defiant. It was a look he was all too familiar with by now. "I'm not afraid of work."

"If you do this, you must go all the way. I will be committing a lot of resources to supporting you. Don't waste my efforts or your own."

"I won't," she promised.

"Stop by Lina's desk and ask her to give you the green folder."

Arabella flashed a smile and took off.

She was a troublesome child, but debts had to be paid. All things considered, she would make a powerful ally in the future. Provided she didn't self-destruct along the way.

Augustine looked out the window again. The sun would rise soon.

Somewhere out there, Diana rested, probably in a bed just like this one.

He missed her.

She told him he was the one. The special one.

The safest course was to pretend it had never happened. Their magic wasn't compatible, their Houses weren't on the same footing, and her nature was too unpredictable for a stable partnership. He recognized all that.

Augustine closed his eyes. He needed to take this time to heal while he could. He needed to be in top shape when he went looking for Diana Harrison, and he wasn't sure how long he could stay away.

ARABELLA SAVES THE DAY

I walked into the gym at a quarter past nine, took my high-heeled cork sandals off—I really liked this pair, they had little blue flowers on them—and crossed the floor.

Gyms were not my favorite places. Something about walls of mirrors and rows of equipment made me feel like I was on display, and I avoided them whenever it was possible. I liked working out—it helped with the stress, and I've had a lot of stress lately—but I preferred doing it where nobody could see me and run away screaming.

Although, as gyms went, this one wasn't too bad. It was large, with a heavy-duty rubberized floor, light and bright, no mirrors, and it was empty except for two people, which was a huge plus.

They stood by one of those heavy, cylindrical punching bags that were designed to take both kicks and punches. The bag hung suspended on a chain from a metal track in the ceiling, and the track ran almost all the way to the back of the gym.

Interesting.

The first person, a muscled guy in his late thirties, carefully pushed the bag forward and stepped to the side. He was a big dude, tall with broad shoulders, a wide chest, and biceps that stretched the sleeves of his black short-sleeved compression tee. His hair looked rough, and he probably knew that but just didn't care. This was the kind of guy who'd rather buzz his own hair off with clippers knowing he would probably miss a spot than sit down for twenty minutes and politely make small talk with a barber.

Ray Braddock. Professional Tough Guy and All-Around Badass.

He kind of reminded me of those high school wrestling coaches who were always super serious and focused and were, like, way too intense at times, but also were helpful, professional, and quietly patient. Until you pissed them off. And then he would be screaming in your face while you just stood there, terrified, watching the blood vessel pop in his forehead and counting the seconds until it was over.

I wasn't here for Ray. I was here to save the other person by the punching bag from the consequences of her actions.

She was seventeen years old, I'd say about four inches taller than me, and dressed in loose red Nike shorts and a basic black sports bra. Tia Madero was built like body fat was afraid of her. All muscle, with visible stomach abs and biceps that had angles and strong, muscular legs. Her dark hair was pulled back into a high ponytail. A few strands had managed to escape, though, and were stuck to her sweaty forehead.

Ray saw me.

The look on his face quickly became the opposite of friendly. Which was weird and, lowkey, a tiny bit concerning, since I didn't look like much of a threat right now. I had chosen my outfit and my style very carefully. Seventeen-year-olds were quick to judge, and I had to get Tia to cooperate. I had to aim for a slightly older sister vibe here: old enough to be taken seriously, young enough to confide in, and fashionable enough not to be dismissed outright. Tia's Insta told me she knew how to apply make-up. She rarely bothered, but when she did it, it looked good enough to pass for being professionally done. I had to measure up.

I had settled on a sleeveless, plaid Burberry dress. My hair, curled and twisted back into a loose bun at the base of my neck, threaded the line between sophisticated and pretty. I paired both with a soft face: taupe eyeshadow, brown mascara, and light blush. My tinted lip-gloss was a nice, very agreeable shade of warm pastel pink. Though apparently less agreeable than I'd thought, since Ray was mad-dogging me across the gym right now.

Ray was Tia's bodyguard. In reality, he mostly got paid to bodyguard everybody else *from* Tia and not so much the other way around. Poor Tia. I'd gotten this case in the middle of the night, and I'd looked at a lot of her pics before going to bed. Most of them had Ray in them, looming behind her with his arms crossed, like a disapproving shadow wearing orthopedic sneakers. Talk about a vibe killer.

Since he was security for House Madero, he'd likely read the files they had on my family. We'd clashed with the Madero clan a few times, so it made sense for the Maderos to keep tabs on House Baylor. My personal records were sealed, which probably made his eye twitch. An unknown threat was always worse. But the fact that I'd walked into this gym on the Madero compound meant that someone with a lot of authority had signed off on it.

It'd been Tia's stepmother. I'd specifically approached her, because if I had gone to Tia's father, Dave Madero would've started the apocalypse.

Our stares connected. Ray locked his jaw.

I gave him a bright smile. *I'm not here to make trouble. Honest.*

Tia saw me, deliberately looked away, and kicked the bag. The heavy bag shot across the gym, sliding on the iron track with a metallic whoosh all the way to the other side of the gym and dangled there.

Nice.

Tia stretched her neck, side to side, her dark ponytail bopping, and nodded. Ray hesitated for a moment. She gave him a look, and he trotted after the bag. Tia turned her back toward me and launched a series of air punches.

She didn't ask why I was here. She had expected someone to show up and ask questions, though. I was on the right track. Now I had to convince her to talk to me.

On paper, I was only three years older than Tia, but the real gap between us was a lot wider. She was a high school junior, and I had already graduated. I was an adult, almost old enough to buy a drink, and she was still a minor. I'd been working for my family's business for years and made my own money, and she still collected an allowance. Most importantly, I participated in House warfare. The Maderos were a violent House. They knew exactly how ugly it could get, and they sheltered Tia from it.

Getting back into the high-school mindset was a struggle. When I was seventeen, other seventeen-year-olds in my life were either angsty or angry. Tia was definitely angry. If I tried to reason with her, she would tell me to fuck off. She was ignoring me right now, so I had to engage her first, and since all I had to work with was anger, I was forced to go with that.

"Hi!" I stuck out my hand. "My name is Arabella Baylor. My brother-in-law fought with your father."

She ignored me.

"And my older sister put your Uncle Frank into the ER," I continued.

She looked at my hand, more specifically at my French-tip nails, snorted, and turned away.

Le sigh. I planned to follow up with, "My other sister's fiancé choked your Uncle Frank with a plastic bag," but her face told me I would have to stab a bit deeper. If I gave her a target for all that rage, she would start talking.

Ray brought the bag back. She spun around and kicked it again.

Thud!

Whooosh!

I gave her a polite, lukewarm golf clap. She turned around and glared at me while Ray went after the bag.

"You know, you'd get an even better workout if you ran after the bag and then kicked it back," I pointed out.

"Don't tell me how to work out," she snapped.

A response. In words even. Clearly, I had hit a nerve. Good to know.

"Just trying to help."

"Don't. You know fuck-all about what I do." She looked at my nails again.

"I bet you've never punched a bag in your life. Just fucking leave."

"It's my manicure, isn't it?"

She spun a kick at the empty air. Then another.

Like chipping at an iceberg with a pick. Eventually I would find a crack.

"You know who never punched a bag in her life? Emelline Lily. And yet for some reason Phillip Dunwoody is still simping all over her Insta."

THUD! Whoosh!

She sent the bag flying right back literally as soon as Ray retrieved it. Dude almost lost his hand.

Tia glared at me. I felt a tiny pinch of guilt, but I was doing it for her own good, because yesterday she left the house to meet Phillip Dunwoody, who until two days ago had been her boyfriend.

Tia returned home. Phillip did not.

Phillip was a lower-end Significant and the son of a Prime ice mage. Their family wasn't a House, but they were well connected and had a solid reputation. They had been frantically looking for him, which was how MII got involved.

For all of her posturing, Tia didn't resort to violence often. Oh, she slapped people here and there when they attacked her, but it took a lot to provoke her. Phillip must've done something.

House Madero was infamous. They were powerful and very hot-tempered. If you looked up "ferocious" on Wikipedia, you'd find their family portrait. In a fight, they altered their bodies, toughening their skin and boosting their strength, and they took the kinds of jobs that often ended with someone dying.

Their family tree was complicated. Their patriarch, Peter Madero, was seventy-six years old. He had one son, who died, leaving behind his own five sons: David, Frank, Roger, and the twins, Ethan and Evan. When David was seventeen, he'd had a situationship with a girl, and she became pregnant. Since they were both in high school, her parents had lost their shit, pulled her out of school, and sent her out of state to live with her grandparents before anybody had a chance to learn about the pregnancy. Dave had had no idea Tia existed until ten years later, when she was dropped on his doorstep because her powers had manifested and her family couldn't control her. Suddenly she gained a great-grandfather, a grandmother, a father, and four very overprotective uncles.

The entire Madero clan thought Tia was a precious treasure. She was the first girl born into the family in four generations, and they weren't quite sure how to deal with that. They were so paranoid that something could happen to her that they home-schooled her until high school. She hadn't even been mentioned in their family registry until last year. If they got wind of this mess with Phillip, they would level half of Houston in retalia-tion. People would get hurt, House Madero would land in scald-ing-hot water, and the guilt would eat Tia alive.

I kept going. "I barely got any sleep last night, because I spent half of it stalking you and Phillip online. I don't get it."

Thud! Whoosh.

"I mean, I get *him*, but I don't understand why you were with him in the first place. You could do so much better."

"You don't know anything about me."

"You would be surprised how much you can find out on socials. This selfie, for example."

I pulled up one of her pics on my phone and showed it to her. She glanced at it and turned away.

"It's a very pretty pic."

It really was. Tia wore a white skater dress with a plunging neckline, all lace and soft pleats. She stood poised against a stone column, holding a small purse with a cartoon girl drawn in pink with two puffs of pink hair on either side of her head. Tia's own hair fell in gentle curls, and her makeup was light and romantic. She looked like she was going to a wedding.

"This is an original Renata dress."

Tia paused for a millisecond.

Ray suddenly came to life. "What does that mean?"

"It was designed by Lucian Brady for his wife, Renata. She was a Magus Hoplomorphosis, like Tia."

And, like Tia, Renata Brady was muscular and broad-shouldered and wanted to look softer.

"This dress is super rare. There are only fourteen Renatas, and they had a tiny run, only ten units for each design."

"How much did you spend?" Ray asked.

"I found it in a thrift shop for fifty bucks," she told him. "They had no idea what it was. Calm down."

"And this bag." I zoomed the picture in on the cartoon girl. "I always liked the pink Poppy-Chan best."

Ray looked at Tia. She groaned.

Ray turned to me. "Is the bag rare?"

"Yes. During the last recession, Coach released a very small run of these bags in Japan. They got a bunch of crap for it, because these are aimed at teenagers, and people complained that it was manipulative and would make kids beg their parents to buy them luxury bags. Coach pulled Poppy-Chan off the market in a year. They hid these so well, even most Coach employees don't know about them."

"Yes, but they're still in the Coach database," Tia said. "If you give them the serial number, they can confirm if it's authentic."

"Tia?" A warning vibrated in Ray's voice.

"Two hundred and twelve bucks on eBay and only because someone else wanted it and kept bidding a dollar over me for, like, hours."

What was it with Ray and the money questions? It wasn't like the Maderos lacked money, and she wasn't spending that much. By most Prime standards, this was pennies.

"See? This tells me a lot about you," I said.

"Like what?" she growled.

"You don't like expensive things. You like rare things—special, secret finds that you have to search for. They make you happy. You like going out in an outfit like that exactly because you know something about it that others don't."

She opened her mouth and closed it.

"Phillip doesn't get it." I scrolled through the comments under the pic, found his, and showed it to her.

what's with the weird bag

She spun away from me. Ray had abandoned the punching bag a few feet short. She marched to it and kicked it hard.

"His family is looking for him," I said. "His mom is losing her mind. They turned his laptop over to me. Did you know that he was a Derek Areston fanboy?"

Derek Areston was an alpha-male bro. He made his money hawking his self-improvement courses and writing books about how testosterone made you rich and sexy.

"Whatever," Tia said.

Ray let out a derisive snarl. "Areston is an asshat."

"Phillip doesn't just follow Areston. He hypes him up on Reddit."

"What?"

I pulled it up on my phone. *"The Vertex Blueprint: Wealth, Women, and Relentless Drive is peak, man. Absolute fucking peak. It's peak, Tia. Peak cringe."*

She marched over and grabbed the phone out of my hand. "PrimeAlphaProtocol? Is that Phillip?"

I nodded.

For a second she looked like she would smash my phone into the ground, then she thrust it back at me and stomped away.

Phew. Crisis averted.

"This is why I don't get it," I told her. "You don't seem like the kind of person who would put up with that. The second-hand embarrassment alone is so much."

"He didn't used to be like that," she squeezed out.

"But he is like that now. I figured out why you broke up with him, by the way. It was this."

I pulled up Emelline Lily's Insta and found the right pic. In it, a willowy girl with long legs and dark hair posed in a short, black bodycon dress. The dress was strategically cut. Three horizontal slashes stretched over her torso, baring wide sections of her tan chest and flat stomach. She was holding a flute of golden liquid that was likely champagne but could pass for cider if someone freaked out about underage drinking. Her makeup was perfect, her eyebrows were razor-precise, and she held her glass while staring pensively at the evening city from a high-rise balcony. The caption said, "A very long day."

"This isn't even a good thirst trap." I shrugged. "Like she barely tried."

Tia pummeled the bag, sinking a flurry of punches. The bag danced, bouncing farther and farther down the rail.

"What the fuck did he do?" Ray growled.

I pulled up the comments and showed it to him.

"'Your body is fire emoji.'" Ray frowned. "A heart. A face with heart eyes. Heart on fire…"

Tia charged at us, her eyes blazing.

"She goes to Heritage, Ray! She sits one row down from me in History. He left that stupid comment about Poppy-Chan, and then he went and slobbered all over her, and the saddest thing is, she doesn't even fucking know he exists. He's probably falling all over himself in her DMs, and she is leaving him on read. He's pathetic. This whole thing is pathetic. He spouts stupid bullshit, he ignores my texts, and now he's embarrassed me in front of the whole fucking school. He embarrassed himself! Everybody saw it. People are making jokes about me. Someone slapped together a meme. Emelline is a princess, Phillip is a chihuahua with a hard-on, and I'm a troll chasing after both of them."

Ouch. That was so brutal. And immature as hell for high school. That was the kind of shit that you would expect from middle school kids.

Ray blinked.

"Yes, I broke up with him!" Tia threw her hands in the air. "Happy now? Is that what you wanted to know?"

"Like I said, I already knew you broke up with him. I figured that out. Emelline posted this pic on Friday. It took you till next morning to see the fallout. On Saturday Phillip locked himself in his room. When the housekeeper came to get him for dinner, he screamed at her to leave him alone and slammed the door in her face. Phillip is a gift. Anyway, the housekeeper didn't hear any raised voices, which tells me that you dumped him by text and refused to take his calls."

Tia stared at me.

"Phillip is reading alpha male books, which tell him that alpha males don't get dumped. He must've spent the whole night blowing up your phone and worn you down. You agreed to meet him, because both of you left your houses a little before noon on Sunday. I know that Phillip drove west on I-10. His phone died en route, probably because he spent the whole night texting and didn't charge it."

She didn't interrupt.

"You already broke up with him, so you should be cooling off, but you're still breathing fire. He did something when you met. Probably something violent and stupid. You came home. He didn't. His car was found on a small rural road north of the highway. It's Monday morning now, you didn't go to school today, and nobody has seen Phillip."

"Tia, what did you do?" Ray asked.

She raised her hand, and he shut up.

"Poor Phillip," she ground out. "His family must've pulled all the strings, because they've got a Prime looking for him. Because he is such a good kid from a respected family."

She must've looked me up at some point.

"Actually, I don't care too much about Phillip," I told her. "It's my job to find him. I care about what happens to you and your family when his family finds out. House warfare is an ugly thing."

"His family isn't a House."

"His aunt married into House Seaton. They're large, wealthy, and powerful. If I don't find Phillip soon, they will drag the cops into it, or, worse, they will accuse you directly of hurting him."

"Because I'm a Madero. Because we solve all of our problems with our fists."

"Yes."

She glared at me.

"Tia, when my evil grandmother needed someone to kidnap my older sister, she went to your House. There is a reason for that. Your House built their reputation punch by punch. When your father finds out that you're being accused of kidnapping or murder, he will explode like a nuclear warhead. He will attack House Seaton and start a feud."

And it would be a really bad feud.

"Look, I'm not trying to lecture you. I'm just telling you like it is: this will blow up and get really nasty. Phillip has already done enough damage. Why let him ruin your family's life? He isn't worth it. Besides, I don't believe for a second that you want something truly bad to happen to him. He is a shithead, but you are not."

Her face frosted over.

Shit. I fucked up. I'd had her for a little while, and now I lost her.

"You're exactly the kind of girl I hate," she said.

Here we go. "What kind of girl do you think I am?"

"The kind of girl Phillip would simp over."

Right for the jugular. "Is that so?"

"I bet you're rich and popular. You've never been picked on in your life. You were probably the queen of Heritage when you went there. I don't know what your magic is, but I'm sure it's something elegant and pretty."

Don't laugh, don't laugh…

"You come here wearing designer clothes with your little manicure, playing at some kind of detective, and you talk to me like you know me. You don't know shit. You have no idea what it's like when people think you're a violent freak. When they watch you non-stop because they expect you to explode and ruin everything. So don't talk to me like you fucking know anything about me."

Inside me, the Beast uncurled, a phantom woven of multi-colored strands, each thread a different aspect of my power. There was only so much screaming I could take.

"Done?" I asked.

"Yeah. We are done here. Feel free to fuck off."

"I didn't go to Heritage. I went to Donovan, and now I have to take Path to College courses, because my grades are shit."

She blinked.

"I had to beg my mother to let me go to Donovan. They'd homeschooled me for a long time because my mother worried I would snap and level the school."

Tia frowned.

"I'll tell you what," I said. "Let's make a bet. You and I spar, and if I win, you'll tell me what you've done with Phillip. If I lose, I'll leave."

Tia laughed. "You're out of your mind. I'll destroy you, and then your House will make a giant deal out of your broken legs. You see that bag? It's full of sand. Ray has to push it back, and he is huffing and puffing after the first five trips. You and I aren't on the same level, Princess Baylor."

You've got that right.

I reached deep inside me and yanked on the thread of magic I wanted. It was a deep, crimson red.

"It's a very nice punching bag," I said.

"Like I told you, not on the same level," Tia snapped. "So—"

I punched the bag. The synthetic leather cylinder shot across the gym like a cannonball. The heavy bag flew to the end of the track, snapped off the chain, and exploded against the far wall in a cloud of sand.

Tia and Ray stared at me, mouths open.

I shrugged my shoulders and smiled. "Any time you're ready, Princess Madero."

THE METAL CISTERN WAS EIGHT FEET TALL AND PROBABLY ABOUT five feet wide. It sat inside an old barn on a farm near Bellville, on a ranch owned by House Madero. Once used as a fermentation tank for wine, the reinforced stainless-steel tank was built to withstand quite a bit of pressure on its own, but Phillip must've really pissed Tia off, because she'd wrapped several metal fence posts around it.

I knocked on the tank. "Phillip?"

Something scrambled inside the tank, and a voice dulled by metal screamed, "Get me out!"

"Let's chat first."

"Are you fucking crazy? Get me out of here! My family--"

"Your family doesn't scare me."

"You—"

"If you would like, I can come back in half an hour after you've calmed down."

He shut up.

I didn't want him to see me. Getting high school guys to listen to you was a struggle in the best of times, and Tia was right. I was the kind of girl that Phillip would simp over, and I looked young enough that he'd probably try. If I let him out right away, Phillip—high-caliber alpha male that he was—would likely say or try something, and I wasn't in the mood for his nonsense. I had to calibrate my strength to spar with Tia, and that fight didn't let me go all out. It was fun, but I was still twitchy. I had pulled over to the side of the road on the way here and yeeted a very large rock to bleed some of it off. The itch was still there, though, and if Phillip irritated me in my current state, I would end up throwing him around like a ragdoll.

Hi, here is your precious offspring, still alive but slightly floppy. Don't worry, broken bones heal in time. Yeah, no.

"Are you still there?" Phillip asked in a small voice.

I needed to sound older, like someone with authority and experience. I would have to channel Nevada for this.

"Much better," I told him. "Let's have a conversation."

"Who are you?"

"Not important. Suppose I let you out. What's the next step?"

"I'm going home!"

"And then?"

"And then my family is going to cut off House Madero's balls."

I brushed the dirt off a nearby bench and sat on it. "I liked your mom. She is very nice and she is very worried about you, so I'm going to give you a little reality check. Your family isn't combat-ready."

"My dad is a Prime!"

If only Beast had a magic thread for patience. "Your dad calibrates industrial cooling for Seaton paint factories. Your family hasn't fought in a feud. Ever."

"So?"

"House Madero is a combat House. Violence is basically their brand. When violence fails, they apply more violence. They are the people other Houses hire to fight their feuds for them."

"They are fucking hicks. I'm not scared of them."

Ugh. "And that right there tells me that you have no experience."

"And you do?"

"I do. My sister once put Frank Madero in the hospital, so I know exactly what I'm talking about."

That and Connor beating the hell out of Tia's dad were the reason Tia's stepmother met with me instead of brushing me off. Apparently, the only way to earn the Maderos' respect was to punch it into them.

"We have friends and alliances. My aunt is from House Seaton! My dad knows people."

This kid was so irritating. "I'm sure he does. I once saw a recording of Dave Madero ripping a person's head off. Picture it in your head. He grabbed a grown man by his neck and twisted the skull off like it was a bottle cap."

Silence.

"You attacked his daughter."

"That's not what happened!"

I picked up one of the fence posts and twisted it in my hands. Annoying. So annoying.

"House Madero knows their rep. They understand that if any violence happens in their vicinity, people will blame them whether they did it or not. All members of House Madero wear bodycams. The cameras activate automatically when the Maderos leave their compound, and turning them off sends an alert to the family. I bet you didn't know that, did you?"

The cistern went quiet.

I pulled up a video on my phone. The recording was paused, and on the screen Phillip, a thin blond kid, was caught in mid-shout, his mouth open and his face weird.

Tia hadn't disabled her bodycam. She also thought I had seen the footage, because she figured out that I'd talked to her stepmother, who had access to it. Mrs. Madero had gotten worried and came to the gym just as we finished our light workout. Tia became heated with her stepmother, and Mrs. Madero explained that she hadn't watched the footage, because she respected her daughter's privacy. Then Tia needed a moment and went to the bathroom for a while. I got my footage and Phillip's location and got out so they could have their family time.

I restarted the recording and turned the sound up.

"Stop! We're not done!"

"We are so done, Phillip. We are over."

"Tia! I said you can't leave! TIA! I said STOP!"

On the screen, a sheet of blue ice shot from Phillip. For a moment it blocked out the view and then Tia's fist smashed into it. Cracks fractured the ice wall. She hit it again, then again, and the ice bubble burst.

"You iced her."

"I didn't hurt her! I just didn't want her to leave!"

"You encased your girlfriend, the person you're supposed to

love and care about, in a block of ice, because she broke it off with you after you embarrassed her in front of everybody."

"I didn't mean..."

"Phillip. This is not high school. This is big-boy, adult shit. You attacked a member of a combat House. There are consequences. This could start a feud. Your mom and dad can't get you out of it, because if this comes out, they will be too busy screaming while Dave Madero twists their heads off."

Silence.

"He can't do that. There are rules," he said finally.

"Oh good. How could I forget that House Madero is famous for their rule-following. Let me explain to you what will happen: this footage goes public. Dave Madero gets his brothers, and the five of them go over to House Seaton. House Seaton views that footage and realizes that you are at fault. Sure, they can feud with the Maderos, but it will be dangerous and expensive. You are not worth it."

"My dad—"

"Will be very upset, but he has to think about your mom and your two brothers. Why should they pay for this mess you made? If Dave is feeling charitable, you will be jailed. Your family will still likely pay a massive restitution."

"She put me in here! Doesn't that count as kidnapping?"

"It does, but I just recorded you saying that you wanted to kidnap her first."

"I didn't!"

I replayed the recording for him. *"I just didn't want her to leave!"*

Silence.

"Why are you doing this to me?" he asked.

"I'm not doing anything. You did all of this to yourself. You didn't even ask me if Tia is okay. Being iced hurts. Ice that cold burns when it touches you. I know you can't feel it, because you're an ice mage, but surely somebody explained that to you before."

I added the second fence post to the first one and knotted it up.

"Is she okay?" he asked.

"No. She is hurt and angry."

More silence.

"Something bad is happening to you, Phillip," I said. "Tia told me that when you first started going out, you were a kind kid. Now you're stalking influencers and reading books written by losers."

"Areston isn't a loser."

"Of course he is. Anybody who has to beat his own drum that hard is a loser. Who is the scariest Prime you can think of?"

"Mad Rogan."

Serendipity. "Do you see Mad Rogan running around Houston telling people how alpha he is? Do you think he's on Herald, talking about peak protocols?"

"That's different."

"How?"

"He is Mad Rogan."

I twisted the fence posts. Metal groaned.

"What is that noise?"

"Don't worry about it. Tia said that when you'd just started dating, she'd had an accident and hid in the bathroom. She didn't know anybody who would help, so she texted you, and you left campus, bought her tampons and a new pair of shorts, and snuck it to her in the girls' bathroom."

Silence.

"*That* Phillip had Tia. This new 'peak' Phillip lost Tia and is now stuck in a cistern, trying to figure out how to keep his family safe from the mess he made."

"What do you want?" he asked. He sounded defeated.

"I want to go home and take a nap. Right now, though, I want to save you from yourself because of that tampon run."

I pulled his phone out of my pocket, stood on my toes, and tossed it through the gap in the top of the cistern, which Tia had left so he wouldn't suffocate. Tia had taken his phone after their fight, and I had confiscated it from her. I also explained to her the pitfalls of keeping evidence that can incriminate you for future reference.

"Look at your texts." I'd charged it on the way to the barn.

There was a short pause. "What?!"

"That's a picture of you with Mad Rogan."

I had called my oldest cousin and sweetly asked him for a favor. Bern's photo manipulation skills were on another level. We'd bargained and agreed that I would bring home his favorite French dip sandwich from Firehouse Subs. He would've done it anyway because I'd asked, but there had to be some pretense of a bribe.

"I don't understand."

"Yesterday Tia broke up with you, so you got upset and talked to your friend, Ragnar Etterson."

Ragnar was probably one of the most popular juniors in Heritage High. He was all the things: handsome, smart, and, most importantly, confident. At some point, Ragnar had cracked the high school popularity code. He was that effortlessly cool kid who didn't seem to need anyone, and people flocked to him. It didn't hurt that he was Prime Venenata. The fact that he could poison the entire school to death in seconds just made him cooler.

"I know who he is…"

I bet you do. "Ragnar felt sorry for you and invited you to a barbeque for his sister Runa, which was being held at the house of Linus Duncan. He is the older man who is posing with you in the fourth picture. Linus told you that you are a bright young man who has potential. Then you and Ragnar snuck into Linus' study, smoked cigars, and tried his whiskey, and then both of you decided that you shouldn't go home like that, so you spent the night with the Ettersons, where I found you today. If your family asks Ragnar about it, he will back you up."

"Why would he do that?"

"Because I asked him to."

I hadn't gone through all this trouble for Phillip's sake. I did it for Tia. Defending yourself was fine, but the moment she stuffed him into that cistern, she opened a whole can of potential criminal charges. The best thing for everyone involved was to sweep this whole disaster under the rug and forget it ever happened.

"When you tell this story to your family, watch your father's face when he hears Linus' name. You will not be in trouble. You will be told not to make your parents worry again, and everything will be fine. If you stick around quietly, you will hear your father call his friends and casually drop that Linus Duncan thinks his son has potential. Ragnar will also say hi to you in school in front of everyone."

"I…"

"This never happened. You never iced Tia. You were never in the cistern. Do you understand?"

"Yes. But if Mad Rogan…"

"Mad Rogan is my brother-in-law."

There was a thud.

I waited. Hopefully he hadn't fainted.

We sat side in silence, me on the bench, with a Gordian knot of fence posts, and he in the cistern.

"Is Tia very angry?" he asked finally.

"Yes."

Silence.

"That relationship is over," I told him. "You ruined it."

"I know."

"You have a choice now: peak Phillip, who is going to tell his family about the evil Maderos, or real Phillip, who will apologize to his ex-girlfriend and try to do better next time he decides to date. I'm tired of sitting here, so you need to decide. What will it be?"

<hr>

TIA RUBBED HER HANDS. THE T-BONE STEAK IN FRONT OF HER was the size of her whole plate. My ribeye was almost as large. It smelled like smoke, and I was trying not to drool. I hadn't had breakfast or lunch.

"May I bring you anything else?" the waiter asked.

"No," Tia told him.

"We're good," I agreed.

The waiter nodded and went away.

We were sitting on the patio of Stag and Ale, one of the best steakhouses in Houston. After that spar, Tia had questions, so I invited her to dinner. Dropping off Phillip had taken a while. It was past seven now, and I was starving.

We cut into our steaks at the same time. Mmmm, meat.

"So why Donovan?" Tia asked, chewing. "Why not Heritage?"

"When I started high school, my family wasn't a House. Heritage wouldn't take me. Also we couldn't afford the tuition. I made a whole tragedy out of it back then."

The steak was delicious.

"How is Donovan?" Tia asked.

"Chill. I liked it."

"Do you think I could transfer?" she asked.

"I don't see why not."

She skewed up her face. "Anything would be better than Heritage at this point."

I texted her Julieta Cabrera's email. "This is their guidance counselor. She is also their registrar. She is super nice. Like, she is the only reason I didn't drop out in my freshman year."

"What happened?"

"I didn't know how to people. I was also angry and got upset over stupid, small shit and then let it spiral me out. Sometimes I would go and just sit in her office. It's so nice. She has scented candles, and it's quiet. It helped me with my temper."

Tia sighed. "Not punching people is hard."

"Yes. I had a real struggle while talking to Phillip. I had to leave him in the cistern for most of the conversation, because I didn't trust myself. How did you put up with him for so long?"

"Like I said, he wasn't like that at first. I was awkward. Those assholes look down on me because of my family and because I'm… I'm me. He was the only one who would talk to me. And then the tampon thing happened."

"What changed, do you think?"

She snorted. "I know exactly what changed. I was there. We were in the lounge waiting for the assembly, and people were talking about House warfare. Seth Floris made a joke. He said that if shit hit the fan, Phillip would be the only one to survive, because he would hide behind me."

"True."

"I know! And Seth didn't mean it in a bad way. We spar sometimes. He was just giving me a compliment. People laughed. Phillip got this weird look, and now four months later he is AlphaBullshitProtocol or whatever that was."

One joke. That's all it took. Wow.

She leaned back and sighed. "I do not want to go back to that school. I just… I can't. And my dad made a big deal out of me going to Heritage."

"Talk to Ms. Cabrera. She will help. If anybody can talk your dad into it, she will do it."

"Thanks," Tia said.

"Any time. Do you mind if I ask you something?"

"Ask."

"What is it with Ray and money questions?"

Tia rolled her eyes. "The Veiled Atelier."

"The gacha game? The one where you buy the outfits?"

She nodded. "They had a special event and I got carried away."

"How carried away?"

"Four thousand dollars."

I almost choked on my steak.

"I was depressed."

"4K worth of depressed?!"

She shrugged. "They've cut my allowance by half until I pay it off. Ray got the worst of it. His job title says bodyguard, but he's more like my nanny. He was supposed to supervise me."

"Did you family expect him to stand over your shoulder and keep you from buying pixels?"

"That's what he said. He got chewed out anyway, so now he is paranoid." Tia raised her head. "What smells so good?"

Something did smell good. Fried and delicious. Where was it coming from... I tugged on my magic, grabbing a silver-blue strand. The world opened like a flower, and the scents flooded in.

"I'm pretty sure it's those fried mushrooms over there."

"We should order some!"

"We should!"

Then a familiar scent floated past me. *Oh no, you don't.*

I put my fork down and pointed at the chair next to me. "In the chair. Right now."

Tia raised her eyebrows.

A small shape slipped out from behind an ornamental shrub. Behind her, a raccoon, a cat, and a Doberman popped into view.

I thought so.

Matilda scurried over and sat in the chair, her animals still poised by the bushes.

"Who is this?" Tia asked.

"My little sister," I told her.

"We are not sisters," Matilda corrected, a serious expression on her face.

Checked by a little kid. "Thanks, Matilda. That hurts my feelings."

"Why? It's true."

Ouch. "Yes, we are not technically sisters, but I love you and think of you as my sister."

"I'm sorry," Matilda said. "I did not mean to hurt your feelings. Would you like to hold Go Min Nam to feel better?"

I glanced at Go Min Nam, who was still sitting by the shrub, looking beyond beautiful with his cream fur and blue eyes. That cat was a prince among all Himalayan felines.

"I would, but I don't think the restaurant would be okay with it."

"Do you forgive me?" Matilda asked.

"Yes."

Matilda turned to Tia. "We do not share biological parents."

"Aha," Tia said.

"But our parents are colleagues and friends, and we care about each other. Father says it is called found family." Matilda reached out and patted my hand. "I also think of you as my sister."

"Thank you."

Tia clearly wanted to ask questions. For a second I thought she would, but she stuffed steak into her mouth instead.

"Matilda, how did you get here?"

"I told Calvin I was meeting you for dinner," she said.

Translation: she'd gotten one of our security guys to drive her.

"So you lied?"

Matilda nodded, her dark hair shifting. "Yes."

"Why did you lie?"

"My aunt isn't answering my texts."

Oh. "Diana is the Head of the House. She might be busy."

"She tells me when she is busy. This morning, she went to see Augustine Montgomery, and now she is not answering my texts. You also go to see Augustine Montgomery. Frequently."

I knew Matilda was spying on us. I just didn't realize how thorough she was.

"Who is this Augustine?" Tia asked.

"I'm doing an internship with MII. He owns MII."

"That tells me nothing."

I pulled up the picture of Augustine poised against the cobalt glass tower of the MII building and showed it to Tia.

Her eyes widened. "Whoa."

"What is an internship?" Matilda asked.

"I work for Augustine investigating cases to get experience."

"Why are you doing an internship?"

"Better question: why am *I* not doing an internship?" Tia muttered.

If she wanted to do an internship with MII, it wouldn't be a bad place. Augustine was super safe to crush on even for high school girls. Not only he was god-tier handsome, but he was also too old and therefore off-limits, and he was 100% above board. He would never creep or lech. And if any of his employees tried something, they would be instantly fired.

Matilda was waiting for my response.

I sighed. "I want to go to a special college. My grades aren't good enough, so I have to work extra to get accepted."

Matilda thought this over. "Why didn't you tell anybody about the internship?"

"You think I didn't tell anybody. You are mistaken. I told Nevada. Ha!"

Matilda frowned. "But you didn't tell Ms. Penelope."

"No." Sometimes talking with Matilda was like conversing

with a very old, sage witch that somehow ended up in the body of a nine-year old.

"Why?"

"My mom hates Augustine and doesn't trust him. If she knew I was doing an internship at MII, she would try to talk me out of it, and then she would stress out about my safety. I don't want her to worry."

Matilda nodded.

"Also, when I was much younger, I told my mom that it was her fault that my grades were bad, because she didn't pay enough attention to me. It wasn't true. My grades were bad because I didn't care. But I was angry at the time, and I didn't want to be in trouble. It upset my mom. I don't want her to know that my grades aren't enough because she might blame herself."

And that just kind of flopped out. Great going, me. It had been eating at me for weeks, ever since I secretly started the Path to College. Here I was, baring my soul to a girl I just met and to Matilda. Awesome. Just awesome. Maybe it was the lack of sleep.

"What's your GPA?" Tia asked.

"3.4."

"That's not bad."

"No. But it's not good enough for what I want to do. It needs to be stellar."

"Why?" Tia asked.

The two of them were looking at me. Well, I started it.

"I have two sisters," I explained. "My oldest sister, Nevada, took over the family business when she was seventeen. She kept us fed, and got a degree, and she is a truthseeker Prime. She is super competent. At everything."

I just kept talking. It felt like a good idea for some reason.

"My second sister is like a super-computer. She can do math in her head. Not like baby math, like the complicated, people's-eyes-go-big kind of math. She is now the Head of House. She thinks in multiple directions. Like I honestly think that she isn't human. Our evil grandmother is Victoria Tremaine."

"Oh shit." Tia set up straighter.

I wasn't surprised she knew who Grandma Victoria was. She was a terrifying legend. People used her to scare their kids at night.

"Catalina managed to contain Victoria Tremaine. She outmaneuvered her."

"I thought we were bad. Your family is fucking scary," Tia said.

"Exactly. Those are my sisters. My cousins also live with us. And, if you ever meet them, and you hear Leon call me sister-cousin, it's because they were officially adopted. He says shit like that because he thinks it's funny. Anyway, Bern, my oldest cousin, can hack any computer and writes programs that make elite coding people weep with envy. Leon shoots around the corners and never misses."

Tia stopped eating. "That's a lot."

"Yeah. And here I am. I get big and smash shit."

Tia put her fork down, reached out, and took my hand. "Hey. I feel that."

"Thanks." I squeezed her hand.

It hit me like a train. I needed a friend. I didn't have one. I had my family, and I had Runa, but she was older and she was dating Bern, which made things slightly complicated.

"I want to accomplish something. Something that has nothing to do with my magic. I want to do it without my family's help. I want to be competent and scary, and I want to take care of my mom and everybody else. I'm not good at a lot of things, but I'm good at business. And I'm good at people and politics. When we have a difficult client who won't pay their bills, I go and talk to them, and I get that payment. Nobody in my family can do that as well as I can. Nevada did okay with it, but she is married now, and honestly, I'm better at it. That's my thing."

I was just having verbal diarrhea now.

"You get the money," Tia said.

"Yes. I realized at some point that unless I could control my temper, I wouldn't ever be able to leave the house because I kept crashing out and getting into fights. So I studied people. I watched them, and I figured out what drives them, so I could manipulate them instead of bashing their faces in. When I came to talk to you today, everything I did—the hair, the makeup, the clothes—was calculated. I could tell you were angry, and I knew that pissing you off even more was the only way to get you to tell me where Phillip was."

I waited for Tia to throw her drink in my face.

She stuck her thumb up. "It worked!"

What?

"Like, it was kind of awesome. Because if they sent anybody else, I wouldn't have told them shit."

Um. "Thank you?"

"You're welcome. Please continue with the rant."

"I'm almost done. I want to get a degree from Rice. I want to double major in Applied Magic Theory and Business Admin. It's not just about academics, though. It's about meeting the right people and getting to know how they think, because down the road they would be our clients and our enemies. I need Augustine for this. First, I need him to write me a letter of recommendation for Rice, because I know that's the only way I can get in. But it's more than that. That dude is a fucking shark. He knows everything about everyone. He's like a surgeon when it comes to House politics. He is *in*. I want him to teach me how to be like him. And right now, he thinks I'm a nuisance. I told him I found Phillip, and he was like, cool, next. And I don't know what else I can do. I guess I will pick up the next case tomorrow and try to impress him again. Thank you for coming to my TED Talk."

Matilda was watching my face.

"You probably didn't get any of that, did you?" I asked her. "Matilda, your Aunt Diana is the Head of your House, just like Augustine is also the Head of his House. The two Houses are allied through a friendship pact. They are probably doing some kind of House business together."

"I'm worried," Matilda said.

"I'm sorry. I will text Augustine after dinner. He won't tell us what he is doing, but maybe he can get your aunt to text you back. Okay?"

"Okay."

"Would you like some ice cream? They have really yummy ice cream here."

Matilda opened her mouth.

My phone chimed. Augustine. I put my finger to my lips and answered, putting the call on speaker.

"Yes?"

"I'm sending you coordinates. If I don't text or call you in two hours, I will need an extraction."

I almost did a double take at the phone.

"I need plausible deniability. Don't use MII resources."

OMG. Here was my chance. "Understood."

Augustine hung up.

I plugged in the coordinates and switched to satellite view. A giant ugly house by Canyon Lake.

I pulled my tablet out of my purse, logged into our database, and typed the address. Tia got up and came to look over my shoulder.

"Adrian Woodward, Prime Animator."

Matilda bared her teeth like an angry kitten. "He tried to buy Zeus."

"He did?"

"Who is Zeus?" Tia asked.

I showed her a picture of Zeus.

"Holy shit."

"Matilda, why did Woodward want Zeus?"

"He wanted Father to keep Zeus still while he cut him apart to study his body."

"Oh, hell no," I told her.

"Yes." Matilda's voice carried a trace of a snarl. "Hell no."

Augustine wouldn't have called unless he expected an extraction. There was a slim chance that he would text me again, but the fact that he involved me meant his back was against the wall. And Diana was likely with him. They were going to attack Woodward.

I got up. "I'm sorry, I've got to go."

"Hey," Tia said. "Do you want some backup?"

"Yes, but this is likely to get violent and messy."

Tia grinned. "My two favorite words."

"I'm coming," Matilda said.

I looked at her.

Matilda opened her eyes wide. "May I also come? I will stay out of the way. I will be useful."

"Are you trying to look cute and pitiful to manipulate me?"

"Yes."

"Good girl. You can also come."

"Is that okay?" Tia asked.

I nodded. "She is an animal Prime. Her family has been taking her to House warfare fights for years. Matilda is small but deadly. Come on, we've got to pay the check, and then I need to call my brother-in-law. I'm going to need to borrow a helicopter."

EXTRAS

These stories previously appeared on our site, Ilona-andrews.com, and are included here as a bonus.

PREFACE

These stories previously appeared on our site, Ilona-andrews.com, and are included here as a bonus.

A MISUNDERSTANDING

S ome days just suck.

First, I found a stain on the cute dress I planned to wear today. Then I spilled my coffee. Then I hit my toe on the door frame to the office. I really wanted to kick the door, but the last time I punched an offending surface, I had to lie to Catalina and claim that a support beam in an abandoned building spontaneously collapsed. If it had been my oldest sister instead of my second oldest sister, I wouldn't have gotten away with it. Nevada knew when you lied to her. Catalina totally believed me.

Lying to Catalina wasn't a habit I cultivated. Oh, I lied casually all the time and never got caught, but lying to Catalina was like kicking a baby deer. It made me feel guilty and I avoided feeling guilty whenever possible. But my family just now relaxed enough to stop continuously worrying I would change my shape and be killed because of it. I didn't want to heap more onto the worry pile.

I was supposed to be working on the case Catalina accepted for a friend, and I was making good progress when Leon called. Leon was my younger cousin. Mom had adopted him and my older cousin, Bern, on account of my aunt being a heinous bitch, and they were more like my brothers. One time I called Bern brother-cousin in public, and then we had to leave the wedding reception for Mom's friend because everyone kept giving us weird looks. It was hilarious.

Leon kept the call short. "I fucked up. Come help me and Grandma. Don't tell Catalina."

I wasn't planning on telling Catalina anything. She had her hands full.

A quick investigation revealed that Grandma Frida was gone and so was the Brick. The armored vehicle was her new baby. She took one of the Humvees we claimed when some idiots attacked our warehouse and spent the last three years turning it into an indestructible monstrosity. She never let any of us drive it, which meant that Leon must've called her first and she took the Brick and went to help him.

Leon had been working the Yarrow case, named so because of the subdivision where the woman he was investigating lived. I didn't know much about it except that the woman worked as an accountant and apparently embezzled money from her friends' businesses. None of that required either Grandma Frida or the Brick.

I jumped into my car and drove to the address he texted.

Yarrow Northwest was a master-planned community in Katy, which was technically its own city west of Houston. In reality, Houston sprawled in all directions, like some giant amoeba that gobbled up the neighboring municipalities. It swallowed Katy a while ago and now there was no way to tell where Houston ended, and Katy began.

The Yarrow boasted about seventy homesites, all featuring EcoSmart technology, large yards, amenities like tennis courts and an onsite waterpark with slides and a lazy river, and prices of a million and a half and up. According to Leon, they actually measured the grass on each lawn with a ruler. It was so trendy, it made me want to spray paint unicorns pooping rainbows in their driveways just to add some life to the place. Buying a house in Yarrow made a statement. *I am successful. Look at my house, look at my beautiful family, look at our lazy river and our precision trimmed lawn and perfect little flowers and despair, for we are better than you.*

Who would want to float in their lazy river anyway?

Logically I could think of some reasons why someone would want to live in a place like that, but it wasn't for me. We worked too hard for our money. When we bought a house, nobody would tell us how long our grass could be, what color we could paint the walls, or where we could park our cars. If I wanted a turret on my roof, I would get a damn turret...

When we bought a house... All of us had been working very hard toward that magical house, but so far we hadn't found a good one. A house would solve a lot of our security problems. The warehouse wasn't defensible, and we were all too old to live together. Bern had to be dying for his own place. Leon, too. Trouble was we needed something large enough for all of us and secure, and while there were plenty of mansions and compounds around Houston, there wasn't much available in our price range. Catalina had gone a little crazy trying to get this taken care of and I watched her closely. We didn't need a repeat of the other incident.

I took the exit, drove up the road to the side street, and took a short drive to the gated entrance of Yarrow. I smiled at the guard in the booth and punched a code into the digital display. The heavy iron gates parted, and I steered the Mercedes through. The guard smiled back as I drove in. The car was fancy enough and I looked the part – a pretty nineteen-year-old blonde in a designer grey dress driving a Mercedes.

"Call Leon."

The phone rang, and my cousin answered through the car's speaker. "Are you almost here?"

"I'm in the neighborhood. Which house is it?"

"Keep going. You'll see it." He hung up.

And that wasn't ominous. At all.

I guided the car down the lane. To the left of me, a beautifully landscaped median offered flowerbeds and picturesque shrubs. To the right, driveways peeled off, each leading to a walled estate secured by an identical gate.

You'll see it.

All the houses looked the same. Some had stucco, some were brick, but at their core, they were all the same, slightly modified version of a McMansion…

The house on my right was missing the gate. That fact took a second to register, and I drove right past it. I reversed and backed up. The gate lay in the inner yard, twisted. Past it, a large vehicle-shaped hole gaped where the front door should have been.

Damn it, Leon.

I turned into the driveway, leaned forward as I drove up to the hole, and peered through the windshield. The interior of the house was darker than the outside, but I saw the unmistakable blocky outline of Brick's rear. The Humvee was *in* the house. The damages. So many damages.

Catalina would kill him. And I would hold him while she bashed his head in.

I shut off the engine and went inside. The place had a wide foyer. Twin staircases hugged the opposite walls, leading upstairs to a unified landing. Two black tire marks stretched from the front door, across the shiny grey marble floor, across a beige oriental rug, all the way to where Brick now waited in front of a steel door. The door looked really out of place in the upscale house and sported a big dent. A panic room. Great.

They had driven the Humvee through the front door, through the foyer, through the sitting room and half of the damn house, and then they rammed it into the steel door.

Damn it. Damn it with sprinkles on top.

Grandma Frida sat on top of Brick looking bored. To the right, a shirtless Leon rested on the floor, leaning against a coffee table that had somehow survived the vehicular assault. His T-shirt, once white and now bloodstained, was wrapped around his head. A white man in his mid-thirties frantically paced back and forth around a white couch as if trying to wear a hole in the rug.

"Have you all lost your minds?" It seemed like a fair question.

Leon pointed to the man. "His fault."

I looked at the man. "Who are you?"

The man stopped pacing and looked at me for the first time. "I'm Kent. Kent Mills. I live here. This is my house."

He was the suspect's spouse.

"What happened?"

Leon gave me an exhausted look. "This is Kent Mills. He works as a registered nurse. This is his house, except it's actually being foreclosed on because his wife, Sandra Mills, who is our suspect, failed to pay the mortgage. For six months."

"I did pay the mortgage!" a woman's voice shrieked through the speaker above the steel door. *"It's a misunderstanding!"*

Kent spun toward the door. "Oh yes, another one of your famous 'misunderstandings.' It's a clerical error, it's a computer glitch, and you'll call them tomorrow and straighten this right out."

"You're a bastard, Kent. A stupid, selfish bastard!"

Kent sucked in a lung full of air.

I used my best impersonation of Mom's voice. "Shut it."

He clicked his mouth closed.

I turned to Leon. "How did Brick get in the house?"

"I'm getting to that. We were hired by The Shaw Distillery to investigate possible embezzlement. I determined that their bookkeeper, Sandra, was robbing them blind."

"That's a lie and I'll sue you for libel," Sandra screamed through the speaker.

"That suit will be thrown out, because it should be slander, not libel," I said. "If you're going to threaten someone, at least do it correctly."

"I looked into the other businesses she did the books for," Leon said. "She befriended people, convinced them to let her handle their books, and then stole everything they had."

"That's another lie. I'm telling you, it's a misunderstanding."

Leon rolled his eyes. "A lie the way your MBA is a lie?"

Kent blinked. "Wait, what? I saw the diploma from UT. It's in the office."

"Fake," Leon said. "She has an Accounting Certificate from Houston Community College. UT has no record of her ever attending."

"It's a –"

"A misunderstanding!" Grandma Frida, Leon, and Kent finished in unison.

"Get to the part where the two of you drove the car into the house."

Grandma Frida drew herself up straight. "It's not a car. It's an armored assault vehicle." She petted Brick's roof. "You don't listen to her. You are a magnificent beast."

I had to strain to not shake my fists at them.

"I found nine businesses she defrauded for a total of eight million dollars," Leon said.

"Eight million? Really?"

"She's been doing it for years."

"Eight million, Sandy, and you couldn't pay the mortgage?!" Kent roared.

"It was fine! It was all fine until you ruined it!"

"Where did the money go?" Kent demanded.

"She bought a winery," Leon said. "Seriously, who does that?"

"Sandy! What the hell do you know about wine?"

"You never believed in me, Kent."

My head began to throb. I rubbed my temples.

Leon heaved a sigh. "I came here to talk and give her a chance to come clean. At that point, Mr. Mills ran out, hysterically screaming that his wife had locked herself in the panic room with his little girl."

A child? These two had a child?

"So you called Grandma, talked her into driving Brick here, and rammed it through the house into the panic room? Do you have any idea the conversation Catalina will have to have with our insurance company?"

Leon waved his arms. "I did my due diligence. First, I had him formally hire us. He signed a waiver absolving us from any liability resulting from damages to the property. Second, I called Grandma. I wanted to go with a blow torch. She decided that, and I quote, 'ramming it is faster.'"

"Grandma!"

She shrugged. "The angle of approach wasn't good. The Brick is wider than the door, so it's hard to hit it right."

"You drove the Brick into the house! And you didn't even break the door."

"How was I supposed to know she'd spent the money on ballistic resistant plate steel?"

"I deserve to have nice things, I work hard, and safety is important to me!"

"I was not consulted about said ramming," Leon said. "I had to dive out of the way and hit my head on this stupid coffee table."

Argh! I wished I could growl but it would just freak everyone out.

"Where is the child now?"

"It's not a child," Grandma Frida said.

Leon passed me a framed photograph. In it, Kent and Sandra held a white Persian cat.

"That's the name of the cat," Leon informed me. "Little Girl."

I turned to Kent. "Why did your wife hide in the panic room?"

Kent waved his arms. "Clint called and screamed at me that Sandra is a scammer, and she bankrupted his bakery. Patrick from the winery had called him, and Clint checked his accounts. I logged into our bank to see if there were any weird deposits and I found that we are broke. It's worse than broke, we are in debt! Our personal credit lines are maxed out. Our mortgage hasn't been paid since August. When I confronted her, she kidnapped my baby and ran into the panic room and now she's threatening to hurt her!"

"Everything was fine until you decided to go digging! I gave you everything, and you just couldn't leave it alone. Why can't you believe me, Kent?"

"You stole from our friends! Everyone knows. Clint and Patrick called everybody! Everyone hates us."

"I made their businesses. Every single one of them was failing until I helped them. They owe me."

Kent looked at me. "I just want my cat back."

"Okay." I walked up to the door. "Mrs. Mills, this is silly. You can't stay in the panic room forever."

"Yes, I can."

"What would you like to happen?" I asked. "What would it take to get you to come out?"

"I want you all to go away. And I want everyone to apologize to me for lying about me. I want Patrick to come here and tell me how sorry he is that he made everyone mad at me."

Denial was a terrible thing.

I tried for my business voice. "Mrs. Mills, that's not realistic. You embezzled a significant amount of money. That's an irrefutable fact provable by financial records and bank statements. No amount of apologies will make it go away."

"What do you people want from me? I do everything. Do you want my blood, is that it? Do you want a blood sacrifice?"

"Nobody wants that. We want you to be healthy and uninjured. Why don't you come out and we can talk about it? I'm sure you were under a great deal of stress. We all make mistakes. As you said, maybe it is all a misunderstanding."

Kent rolled his eyes. Leon made money counting gestures.

"You know what I think?" Sandra asked, a vicious note in her voice. *"I think you're a conniving little bitch. You can tell that bastard that I will break every bone in his piece of shit cat's body. He loves her more than me anyway."*

Who wouldn't? I looked at the door. It seemed standard: solid, with a wheel that rotated, and probably multiple steel bars that secured it when the wheel was turned. Once she locked it from the inside, the wheel wouldn't move.

"Leon, call Sgt. Munoz and let him know that we are about to have an incident. I need all of you to leave the building and not peek. I want to have a private conversation with Sandra."

They looked at me.

"Do you want her out of that room or not?" I made shooing motions with my hands. "Go on."

"I want to…" Kent started.

"Please leave. Your baby is counting on you."

I watched the three of them walk out of the building. The thing about metamorphosis mages was that everyone thought we were one trick ponies. We turned into monsters and sometimes went nuts. But there was more to it. So much more.

I pulled on my magic. It tried to bury me like an avalanche, a glowing mess of rainbow colors, churning together. I picked just one, the dark red one, and let it fill me. The blood-red shadow of the Beast that was my other form filled my mind, colossal, shaggy, with eyes that glowed pure white.

"You wouldn't really hurt a little cat, would you?" I stretched my shoulders.

"Watch me!"

"Have it your way."

I gripped the wheel and strained. In my head the Beast roared. Metal snapped with a sharp clang inside the door. The wheel gave with a grinding noise, the bars slid back, and I yanked the door open.

Sandra Mills stared at me with freaked out eyes. She was white and thin, in her early thirties, with salon-dyed blonde hair and too much foundation that was two shades too yellow for her skin tone. Her sweatpants and an over-sized T-shirt hung on her bony shoulders. She clutched a white cat to her.

She opened her mouth. Nothing came out.

I reached over, grabbed the wheel, and snapped it off the door.

Sandra jerked back.

"I talked to you, and you came out on your own," I told her. "If you say anything different..." I bent the wheel's spokes with my hands.

She nodded frantically.

In the distance a police siren wailed, getting closer.

The Beast evaporated from my mind, as if swept by a wind. Fatigue took over. I winked at Sandra, took the cat from her arms, and headed outside. I would have to spin a cute story for the cops, convince Leon and Grandma that the door must've been damaged by the Brick, and then I would have to call the insurance company. Catalina didn't need one more headache.

I was the youngest kid in my family, but I was a Baylor. We always pulled our weight.

THE COOL AUNT

I leaned toward the mirror and traced my lips with Les Beiges Healthy Glow Balm from Chanel. When you had big eyes and plump lips, you had to pick which one you drew attention to. My eyes were a light blue, the color most people achieved with contact lenses, and once I was done with eyeshadow and mascara, they popped. Any bright shade of lipstick took my face from pretty straight to clown. There were no stops in between. But the medium shade of the Chanel's balm turned out to be my perfect pink. Not too much, not too little, just enough.

Somebody was running down the hall like a small rhino. That was neither new nor unusual in our house. I ignored it and concentrated on contouring my top lip.

Catalina burst into the bathroom. "Nevada's in labor!"

I dropped my balm into the sink. My oldest sister was due any day. Today was a really bad day. Catalina had found some sort of monster construct in the Pit, a flooded area of Houston. I was reasonably sure that she and Mr. Dreamboat, otherwise known as Alessandro Sagredo, her handsome Italian assassin/not-boyfriend, would go there today to kill it. I planned to help. What's better than a monster? A bigger monster.

I was also reasonably sure that Stephen Jiang would be there. Which was why I was taking my time putting on my face.

"The thing in the Pit grabbed one of the Primes and is attacking the work site," Catalina barked. "I have to go. Yesterday, Victoria threatened Nevada and the baby. Go with her and don't let her out of your sight. If it all goes to shit, I don't care if you are in the middle of that damn building, you transform, and you get them out of there."

Change of plans.

This was the first baby for Nevada and for Connor. If I knew anything about my brother-in-law, he would overreact. That meant they wouldn't take a car. They would take a helicopter. If I didn't get a move on, he would stuff her into that helicopter and take off without me.

I pushed past Catalina and sprinted to my room to get my shoes and my purse.

In five seconds, I located four shoes. None of them matched. The only matching pair was the hideous pink crocs, which I wore when my feet hurt from high heels and nobody important could see me. Well, if I did transform, none of my good shoes would be ruined. I stuck my feet into the crocs, swiped the tiny purse with my wallet off the door handle, ran back to the bathroom to get my phone, which I had forgotten, because my sister had come in shrieking like a banshee, and dashed outside.

I got there just as Connor half-helped, half-lifted my oldest sister into the Bell AH-3 Cobra. Some people owned luxury cars. Mad Rogan owned the latest model twin engine attack helicopters. Paranoid rich Primes had the best toys.

Connor saw me running toward them and waved for me to hurry up. I made it to the helicopter and climbed inside. Mom was already there, next to Nevada. I wedged into the seat between them. Connor hopped in, made sure we were all strapped in, and then we were off.

The inside of the helicopter was loud. Connor passed out headsets with mics. I had one just like it for Battlefield Glory, so I could hear the people on my squad as we murdered the Alien Crimson Armada. Cool.

My brother-in-law leaned forward toward Nevada. "Does it hurt?"

She shook her head.

It hurt. I could tell it did by the stony expression on her face. It was the patented Baylor family look that meant yes, it fucking hurts, there is nothing to be done, stop asking me about it. Connor recognized it too because his face went flat. He reached out and took her hand.

"Why are we going to the hospital?" I asked. "What happened to the give-birth-at-your-house plan? I liked that plan."

I didn't like hospitals. Nothing good ever happened there.

"It's a high risk Prime/Prime pregnancy," Nevada said.

"What does that mean?"

"It means the baby is using his magic. He's aware," Mom said. "Being born is scary. We don't know how he will react."

"But you gave birth to all of us and we were fine." We were all Primes.

Mom blinked.

"You almost killed Mom," Nevada told me. "You wedged yourself in and refused to be born."

"What?"

"And the doctor. They pulled you out and you choked him. It took three people to pry you free."

"You're making this up!" I turned to Mom.

She had this weird expression on her face.

It was true. "Mom! You never told me!"

"You never asked. We were very lucky you didn't transform in-utero."

How would anyone know to ask about something like that?

"The difference is, none of us were empathic," Nevada said. "And none of us were using our magic in the womb."

"There is a good chance that our son is empathic," Connor said. "He's linked to Nevada's feelings. Sedation is out of the question. So is the Caesarean."

"Even if they counter the pain with a spinal block and I remain completely calm," Nevada said, "Empathic babies are almost always severely traumatized by a C-section. We don't understand why, but we're not going to risk it."

Connor was a Prime Telekinetic with slight empathic powers, which I didn't ask too much about, because when I looked him up on Herald, the social network for Prime groupies and gossips, the consensus said it was some kind of sexual thing. I didn't want to know what sexual things my sister's husband did. There were boundaries.

Most of the time Primes married within their type of magic. Pyrokinetics married other pyrokinetics, animator mages married other animator mages and so on. Nevada's and Connor's talents were wildly different. Nobody could predict what their baby would be like. The speculation on Herald ran rampant. I've found over seventy threads discussing it.

We knew the baby was telekinetic, because some of his powers leaked to Nevada, giving her temporary telekinetic abilities. According to Connor, that also meant that the baby was a Prime, and with the caliber of his parents' magic, he wouldn't just be a Prime. His power would be off the charts.

It was perfectly possible that Connor's empathic talent made it over to their baby and got a boost from my sister's mental abilities. Which meant a Prime telekinetic with no control over his magic, and possibly capable of leveling a building with a flick of his finger, was about to be squeezed, grabbed, and ejected out of his warm shelter while bathing in psychic pain and anxiety from his mother. If she went into full blown labor in the helicopter…

Oh my God.

"Can this thing go any faster? Make it fly faster."

Mom wrapped her arm around my shoulders. "Calm down."

"You don't understand. I don't have enough hands to catch everyone."

"If the helicopter goes down," Connor said, "Catch Nevada first."

Nevada turned to me. She was wearing that older sister expression that said, "stop freaking out, the adults got this." It used to drive me nuts, but right now it was like a soothing cold shower on my raw nerves.

"The contractions aren't that strong yet. Wait. We will be there in a minute."

I shut up and willed the Cobra to fly as fast as it could.

WE LANDED ON THE HOSPITAL'S ROOFTOP HELIPAD. A DOZEN people waited for us, six in tactical gear armed with automatic weapons, and the others in identical baby blue scrubs. Did they coordinate this? If Nevada was giving birth to a girl, would they have showed up in pink scrubs? Somehow, I had a problem with it, but I couldn't quite put it into words, and I had bigger issues to worry about.

They loaded Nevada into a wheelchair, and we all rushed in a herd into a big freight elevator. It went down and almost immediately stopped. The doors slid open, revealing a hospital hallway with walls painted in pale cream. An announcement echoed, a pre-recorded artificially calm female voice pronouncing the words with crisp precision.

"Code PPB. All non-essential personnel clear the 17th floor."

We made a left out of the elevator and sped down the

hallway toward metal doors that looked like they'd come out of a space station and had been used to contain violent space monsters.

"Code PPB. All non-essential personnel clear the 17th floor."

Nevada exhaled.

"Contractions?" Connor asked.

She nodded.

The doors slid open, we passed through, and they sealed shut behind us. Two of the security people peeled off from our group and stayed behind. I glanced over my shoulder. One of them keyed a code into the door lock. The lights on the door turned red. A metal bar pointing toward the ceiling – that I thought was just a weird part of the door - rotated forty-five degrees before the other guard locked it in place. If someone tried to force the door apart, they would have to rip through the bar to do it.

Could they have made this more dramatic?

A second set of doors slid open. We passed through them, shedding another pair of guards, and the speaker's robotic voice vanished, cut off mid-word.

We came to a T-section, where a hallway crossed ours. The way ahead was blocked by a third door. You've got to be kidding me.

Nevada looked at Connor. "Are we expecting an assault? Is there something you forgot to tell me?"

"Standard procedure," he said.

Most of the medical personnel with us split up, moving into the side hallways. Only two female nurses remained.

The doors in front of us whispered open. We went through, and this time the two security dudes stayed on the other side.

We entered a large round room. The walls were a smooth pale concrete, the floor also concrete in warm tones of brown and beige. It looked like the inside of a bunker. The air smelled of lemon and lavender.

In the middle of the round bunker-room was another room, positioned perfectly in the center, no doors, only two doorways. We rolled through one of the doorways into what looked like an ordinary hospital room. Soothing blue walls, weird medical equipment, most of it bolted to the floor or the walls, a space-age hospital bed, a big screen embedded in the wall near the ceiling opposite the bed, everything seemed almost normal for a high-tech hospital.

In the wall to the right, another doorway offered access to the bathroom. No door again, only a curtain hanging from a rod embedded in the doorway.

Nevada looked at Connor. "Why aren't there any doors?"

"Less things to fly around," he said.

Yeah, also if the doctor and nurses had to run out in a hurry, not having a door helped.

The nurses moved Nevada from the chair onto the bed and started saying soothing words and checking things between her legs.

I reached for my magic. It swirled in my mind, a riot of colors. I plucked at the blue one and let it settle over me. The cobalt image of the Beast, huge and shaggy, crouched in my mind, waiting, staring out through my eyes. I inhaled. The world blossomed into a kaleidoscope of scents. Gun oil, metal, disinfectant, medicinal alcohol, skin cells, deodorant, perfume, soap...

"There are eighteen people in the hallway around this room." Were there cameras in here too? Because if there were, my sister deserved to know she would be on display.

Nevada looked at Connor again. "You said a medical team and a few security people. You didn't say South by Southwest."

A doctor walked into the room. She was about Mom's age, curvy, with large kind eyes, dark brown skin, and a pair of red-framed glasses on her nose. "Hello. I'm Dr. Maier. I'm here to help you."

There was something so reassuring about the way she spoke.

"I'm a Prime laborist, which means I specialize in High Risk Prime Parturition. I've been doing this for twenty years."

"Has anyone ever died?" I asked.

Mom gave me her scary stare. Well, nobody else was going to ask and it was kind of important.

"Yes," Dr. Maier said. "Out of sixty-seven P/P births I've lost two babies and three mothers."

I typed average mortality Prime/Prime Birth into my phone. "It says here the national death rate of P/P births is twenty-eight percent."

"Stop," Mom snapped. "Or I'll take you out of here."

"They should know."

"And trauma to the newborn occurs thirty-two percent of the time," Nevada said. "I do know. Connor and I looked it up."

Oh.

Nevada turned to the doctor. "Thank you for helping me."

"I know it's scary and this is an odd place to give birth, but this is the safest way for you and the baby. This is not our first time. We've done this before. Trust us. We'll take good care of you."

"Why are there so many people?" Connor asked.

"We have an emergency telekinetic team standing by."

"That won't be necessary," Connor said. "I'll contain it."

"The father isn't always the best person," Dr. Maier said.

"In this case, I am the best person," the Scourge of Mexico informed her.

"Very well." Dr. Maier picked up a remote and clicked it. Several people appeared on the screen across from the bed. "These are our halcyons. They're here to keep you and the baby calm. They can't see you; they can only feel your mind. And they're telling me that you're not letting them in."

Halcyons were psionics in reverse. While psionics incited

survival emotions, like fear and anger, halcyons soothed and calmed.

"If you let them alter your mood, it might make things easier."

"I don't think I can," Nevada said.

She had protected her mind for years now. The shields on it were just too thick.

"Okay," Dr. Maier said. "Then we'll proceed without them or the telekinetics. The only people who can see you are in this room. Nothing is being recorded. And if at any point you want someone to leave, tell me and they're gone."

Ten minutes later we knew two things. First, Nevada was almost fully dilated, which was some sort of hell term I didn't want to contemplate. Second, there would be no pain killers. Apparently, my sister had nerves of steel, because the contractions had been coming and she'd kept it to herself and now it was too late for an epidural.

They inserted an IV into Nevada, put a blood pressure cuff on her arm, and put a thing on her belly to monitor the baby's fetal heartbeat. My sister looked slightly lost. Nevada never looked lost. She always had everything under control, even when she didn't.

I came over and hugged her. "If you push too hard, and the baby shoots out like a cannon ball, I promise I'll catch him."

She smiled at me, but her eyes stayed haunted.

The nurses adjusted things. The doctor checked her again. And then Nevada started pushing. Mom held her hand. There were three pushes per contraction. She would push to a count of ten and then relax. Push and relax.

This went on and on. At some point I decided to play on my phone.

We were about two hours into it when Nevada gripped Connor's hand and screamed, and the tv screen shattered. The shards shot out, froze in mid-air, and neatly deposited themselves in the plastic bin.

"I've got you," Connor promised her. "I've got you."

Doctor Maier checked Nevada. "And we have crowning. Break the bed for delivery."

The nurse helped position Nevada's legs into the stirrups and then the bottom half of the bed slid down. Dr. Maier put on a gown and gloves and parked herself between Nevada's legs. I didn't want to look.

The bed jerked to the side and gently slid back.

Nevada growled.

"Perhaps the halcyons..." one of the nurses said.

"Fuck the halcyons," my sister snarled.

"You're doing great," Dr. Maier assured her. "And push."

Nevada strained and relaxed. The fetal monitor made a small noise.

"Why is the baby's heart rate rising?" my sister's voice spiked.

"This is normal," Dr. Maier told her. "Accelerated heartbeat means a happy baby. The heart rate decelerates and accelerates during labor, but everything I'm seeing is within normal levels. Stay calm."

Another contraction gripped Nevada. The fetal contraption beeped. A medical monitor tore from the wall and hurtled towards me, freezing three feet from my head. It hovered there for a second then streaked into the waste bin.

The room turned into a horror movie set. Nevada screaming, fetal monitor going haywire, things flying around, equipment exploding, and my brother-in-law standing in the middle of the chaos, catching things with his mind and holding Nevada's right hand, while Mom held her left, and the doctor kept assuring my sister that everything was going as planned.

I hid by the side of the bed, next to Mom. It seemed like the safest spot.

It kept going and going.

I snuck a peek. Sweat drenched Nevada. She was breathing like she had run a marathon. Connor's face turned bloodless, and I couldn't tell if he was exhausted or worried.

Nevada's gaze met mine.

"You're doing great," I squeaked.

Above us, the ceiling cracked.

Just let it be over. Please let it be over. Please let everyone be okay.

"Almost there," the doctor crooned. "One big push. One more."

Nevada whimpered. The wall behind her shattered. The pieces hung in mid-air caught by Connor's magic.

"One more," Dr. Maier prompted.

"You keep saying one more…"

Nevada's voice was so weak. I'd never heard her sound like that. What if she was dying? She couldn't be dying.

A nurse blotted her forehead. "Almost done, sweetie."

"And.. push."

Nevada strained, moaning.

"There you go," Dr. Maier said. "And the head is out. One more time. This is the last one, I promise."

My sister screamed. A huge crack split the wall and the floor. The room shook. I shut my eyes.

A baby cried. I looked up and saw him, red and wrinkled, smeared with some sort of goo. He had dark hair and he sounded just like a sad kitten who needed to be rescued.

Suddenly things stopped moving. Nevada slumped on the bed.

Connor kissed her. "You did it."

"Is he okay?" she asked.

"He's fine," Dr. Maier told her. "A perfectly healthy boy."

I sagged against the wall. I was never, ever getting pregnant. Ever.

THE ROOM WAS SHROUDED IN A COMFORTING GLOOM. A TABLE lamp in the corner glowed with a soft yellow light. Nevada was asleep on the bed. I saw how much blood came out of her. I still couldn't believe she was breathing. The first time she dozed off, I had poked her to make sure she hadn't died.

Connor slept in a chair. I had a feeling he also thought Nevada was going to die. As soon as she fell asleep, he passed out.

Mom had gone home. After the baby was born, Catalina came in all bloody and glassy eyed. Mom talked to Alessandro and something bad must have happened to my other sister, because Mom decided to take her home. Poor Mom. First, Nevada gave the apocalypse birth, and then Catalina shuffled in like a zombie. This was one of the rare moments when I was the good kid.

My nephew napped in the crib next to his mom. He was all cleaned up, and now he sort of resembled a baby. On a scale of angel to hellspawn, yeah, I had seen cuter babies. Obviously, I didn't say anything, but I did sort of ask Mom if he would look a little less alien later. She told me to give it a week.

A nurse came in and reached for the baby. Connor awoke. He didn't say anything, he just opened his eyes.

"I'll bring him right back," the nurse said and carried him off.

They had been taking the baby out for different medical things, and Connor always went with them. He looked so tired.

I got up and told him quietly, "I've got this one. Rest."

He looked about to argue, but I was already moving.

The nurse hurried down the hallway, two of Connor's security guys trailing her. She ducked into a room on the left, and the guards turned to follow her and stopped at the doorway, with identical blank looks on their faces.

Oh no you don't.

I sped up, pulling on the blue aspect again. Three people besides the baby and the nurse… Wait a minute.

Ha!

I moved silently, sliding behind the catatonic guards. An older man, an older woman, and a scary guy in a suit.

My evil grandmother cradled her great grandchild. The older man next to her practically glowed with pride.

Well, imagine that. That certainly cleared some things up.

"What a beautiful boy," Victoria Tremaine purred. "What a lovely, lovely boy."

The older man smiled.

My evil grandmother rocked the baby. "Look, Trevor, isn't he the most beautiful child you've ever seen?"

"Yes, ma'am. He is," the man in the suit said.

I let them have a few more minutes and walked into the room.

"Grandmother, Grandfather, scary guy I don't know, I'll take the baby now."

Victoria narrowed her eyes at me. I held out my arms. She sighed and passed the baby to me. He squirmed and made a cat noise.

"Support the head," Grandmother said.

"I know."

"We will not speak of this," my grandfather said.

I gave him a big smile. "That will depend entirely on you."

I walked back to the room, cradling my nephew. He was so tiny. And kind of cute.

"Don't worry," I told him softly, snuggling him closer. "I'm the cool aunt. I won't let anything bad happen to you.

The baby looked back at me with big round eyes and farted.

MARTY

I stopped in the doorway of Father's office. He was checking his computer screen and writing something down on a piece of paper. His face was calm and collected, his eyes focused. Floof curled by his feet, snoring softly in a pile of crumpled papers. The plumpy raccoon thought the office was her lair. I bought her a nice kitty bed, but she kept taking paper trash out of the waste basket and making a bed with it instead.

Father was busy, which was nothing new. He was often busy. He liked to say that it was because we needed the money, but I knew the real reason. He missed Mother. He felt helpless when she died, and now he wanted to make sure he was there to do something when other people felt helpless.

I couldn't remember her face anymore. When I tried to recall what my mother looked like, I got a warm, soft smudge with dark hair. I wasn't sure if I was supposed to feel sad about it or if it was better this way. Death was the final predator, and sometimes it pounced when you least expected it. There was no fighting it, but Father still tried and I did, too.

Floof finally caught my scent. She uncurled, rolled onto her feet, and scurried over. I crouched and scratched behind her left ear. She grabbed my leggings with her hands and pulled at the fabric.

Father looked up and smiled. He was always very handsome, but especially when he smiled.

"I have a problem," I said.

"How can I help?"

"It's Marty. He's stuck."

Father got up. "Let's get him unstuck."

We left the office and went down a sunlit path toward the armory. Around us, life hummed. Birds sang. Insects chirped in the ornamental shrubs. Mice scurried, hidden by the flowers in the flower beds.

We turned onto the main "street" of the Compound, a wide, paved road that connected the main gate with the main house. Tall oaks flanked the road, their canopies meeting over our heads, and two squirrels bickered in their branches while three others watched. Squirrels were territorial creatures, and they got into disputes over trees and food and had to have words.

I, too, was a territorial creature. The Baylor Compound was my kingdom. I knew it like the back of my hand. I never fully understood that expression. Was the back of the hand the palm side or the other side...

"Matilda?"

"Yes, Father?"

"Would you like a tutor to help you learn Spanish?"

The C on my test had come back to haunt me. "I don't think that will help."

"What would help?"

"Not learning Spanish."

Father smiled. "You must learn a foreign language. The State requires it."

"I already speak enough languages."

"Oh?"

"Human language, mouse language, racoon language, wolf language, panther language, Tigrionex…"

"I could make arrangements with the school to switch you to the Korean language class."

Mother was Korean. I understood that people assigned a lot of importance to heritage and I was part Korean, so it was my heritage. But learning Korean would hurt, because I would be thinking about Mother the entire time.

"I will try to do better in Spanish."

"Was my suggestion painful?" Father asked.

"Yes. Learning Korean feels unsafe."

"I'm sorry."

"It's okay."

I reached out. Father took my hand, and we squeezed our fingers.

The armory came into view, a fortified building with a construction crew around it. The building had been damaged in the last attack, and Catalina decided that since we had to repair it anyway, we might as well remodel it to better suit our needs.

I led Father to the side of the building where Luis the Electrician stood by a narrow pipe sticking out of the ground. Luis had a long-suffering expression on his face. The first few times I saw him, I asked if he required assistance, but now I knew: Luis thought life was difficult and he always looked that way.

"Is Marty in the pipe?" Father asked.

I nodded. "The building's wires were run through narrow pipes, which turn. Luis has to rewire it, so I attached the wire to Marty's harness. He did two pipes, and this is the third. He went in and he won't come out."

It wasn't that Marty was lazy. He was stubborn. Sometimes he just decided that whatever he was doing was too much work and stopped doing it.

"Did you prompt?" Father asked.

"Yes."

"Try it one more time."

I flicked my animal bond on. It was always there, attached to me like an invisible thread, but now I picked the thread up and tugged on it. On the other end of it, Marty scooted deeper into the pipe. His mind was so quick, and his little thoughts bounced around in all directions, as if you took a cup full of hard plastic beads and emptied it out onto the table.

I visualized treats and sent them down the thread.

Juicy mealworms.

Delicious boiled egg, with the shell half peeled.

Piece of chicken breast, still moist from being baked and dripping with delectable juices.

Nope. Marty stayed right where he was.

I looked at Father.

"Let me try."

I let go of the thread, letting it disconnect. Father closed his eyes.

Seconds ticked by. A tufted titmouse landed on the branch of a nearby tree and tugged on me, wanting birdseed. The feeder was empty.

Marty popped out of the pipe, his pale, cream-colored fur sleeked back. He dashed to Father, wire still attached to his harness, climbed him like a tree, and wrapped himself around Father's neck, nuzzling his cheek with his cute ferret nose and bit him gently. When ferrets loved you, they used their teeth to show it.

"How?"

Father brushed Marty's fur with his fingertips. "Marty was born on a ferret farm. It was a terrible place, run by an evil person who only cared about selling baby ferrets. He didn't take care of his animals. He starved them and let them live in filth. Marty was kept in a tiny cage with his siblings, and when animal control came in and rescued him, he was the only kit left alive in his cage. Marty refused to take food. The ferret rescue people didn't think he would survive, and they called me as a last resort. I tried everything to get him to eat, but he simply wouldn't."

"You never told me."

Marty had appeared in our house two years ago, after I came back from vacation with my aunt. He seemed just like any other baby ferret: hyper, happy, and sweet.

"I didn't tell you about it, because you were still young and it would have upset you."

"Father, I was eight years old."

Father smiled.

Marty slapped father with his paw and dooked, letting out an excited chitter.

"Like I said, you were young and I didn't want to upset you. I was out of options, so I carried Marty everywhere in my sweatshirt, and I would offer him little tidbits of food. One night I was very tired, and I fell asleep. I woke up, and Marty was gone. I followed the bond and found him in Cordelia's enclosure."

Oh. Two years ago, Cordelia and Go Mi Nam had their kittens.

"He was snuggled up against Cordelia. She was cleaning him, and he was eating canned kitten food." Father smiled and stroked Marty's back. "He can't have it too often, since it doesn't have the right combination of nutrients, but once in a while I give it to him as a treat. With Marty, kitten food is a sure bet. I always keep some in my desk."

It must have been so nice for him to curl up against Cordelia. She was warm, fluffy, and kind. Marty must've known that she wasn't his mother, but he needed to feel loved and safe, and Cordelia was very good at loving her kittens.

We detached the wire from Marty's harness. No more pipes required rewiring, so we went back to the office.

Mother was gone, but Father was still here. And my aunt Diana loved me very much. My uncle loved me, too. He didn't like people. He was mostly a wolf himself, but he knew I was family. If I was in trouble, he would come to help me and he would kill anyone who tried to hurt me.

I had the Baylors. Everyone took care of me. If I wanted love, I didn't have to look very far.

"I think I would like to try learning Korean," I said.

"Are you sure?"

"Yes."

"If it becomes painful, please don't force yourself."

"I won't."

I moved closer to Father. He hugged me, and his arms were warm and safe. I smiled at him and we went back to the office to reward Marty with kitten food.

INN TALKS

While we do not have a multiverse, sometimes our characters end up at Gertrude Hunt, a bed-and-breakfast inn that caters to a very particular type of customer. They enjoy delicious snacks, prepared by a chef who was once fired in connection with poisoning of some Galactic royalty, and talk about their lives.

ARABELLA BAYLOR

Dear readers, welcome to Gertrude Hunt for this edition of Inn Talks. Today, by popular demand, we have a special guest, Arabella Baylor of House Baylor.

Arabella: Thank you for having me. The tea is delicious.

Dina: It's our pleasure.

Arabella: Also, the little pastries with the strawberry filling are to die for.

Dina: I'm so glad you like it. I'll let our chef know. He'll be delighted. So, I have a checklist of things to ask you.

Arabella: Oh no. It's getting serious.

Dina: We pride ourselves on being thorough. So first, you look very well put together. What are you wearing?

Arabella: Nothing too special today. The skirt is the cherry miniskirt from AKNVAS, multi-colored plaid, high-waisted, front-slant pockets. The pockets are functional which is my favorite thing. Also, since I'm short, the mini hits a little lower on my legs, which is great for business settings. The matching Valdi blazer is from the same brand. The white turtleneck I picked up at JC Penney's for about $20.

Dina: Are clothes important?

Arabella: Very.

Dina: Why?

Arabella: Well, the obvious reason is that I want to look cute. I mean, we all want to look cute. As you know, I come from a very large but tight-knit family. We own an investigative agency. Prior to becoming a House, we mostly handled insurance fraud, some bail jumpers, cheating spouses, and so on. Small time non-violent offenses. Now our business revolves around the magical heavyweights of Houston. Our clients come from dynasties several generations deep. The sort of people who custom order baby apparel from a couture shop in France and have it flown in by a special courier. One must fit in to be taken seriously, especially since they usually see me when the bill comes due.

Dina: What kind of cases are you typically handling now?

Arabella: A lot of theft, both physical and IP. Fraud is very common, usually within the bounds of the family. A large sum of money disappears, and the Head of the House wants to know which one of their siblings or offspring is responsible. Background checks are huge, the kind that go beyond the basic databases. Still catch a lot of cheating spouses, though. Hehe.

Dina: Some things never change no matter how much money you make?

Arabella: Exactly. But to go back to your earlier question about clothes. It's not just clothes. My hair is done, my makeup is on point. My nails are manicured. When my older sister, Catalina, throws on some sweatpants and trudges out in the morning to walk Shadow with her hair messed up and black circles under her eyes because she stayed up too late working on some thorny Warden case, nobody is alarmed. Everyone in the family knows that Catalina's specialty is maintaining steel control over her magic. I don't have that same luxury.

When everyone around you is paranoid that you might Godzilla-out at any second, you try to compensate. When I was younger, I'd adopt over-the-top cute mannerisms and get into funny fights where I would flail harmlessly to reassure everyone that I was in control. Now I accomplish it with this. ::indicates the outfit:: I'm the antithesis of frazzled. I'm composed and elegant, and in control. Do you know how much bearing sloppy clothes and unbrushed hair has on my potential to explode?

Dina: How much?

Arabella: None at all. What I look like is not an indicator of how I feel in any way. However, people can't help but make visual judgements. Even when they are your family, and they love you.

Dina: Speaking of family, is it true that you once said that you're nobody's favorite?

Arabella: I knew as soon as I said it that it would come back to haunt me. But I stand by it. I don't want to give anyone the wrong impression. I'm loved. My family is supportive and caring. And I wasn't treated any differently than my sisters when it came to gifts, chores, or attending school functions. But some things are subconscious.

Nevada is Grandma Frida's favorite. She is the first grand-child. Grandma Frida still calls her "the baby." I used to have a lot of butthurt over that. I'm the youngest. I should be the baby.

Both Grandpa Linus and Grandmother Victoria prefer Catalina. Grandpa does dote on me. I can come to him for advice any time, and he spoils me. But he doesn't respect me. He doesn't take me seriously. I'm humored. Grandmother Victoria mostly doesn't notice I exist, unless I specifically get her atten-tion. To be fair, she ignores Nevada and my cousins as well. She put all of her eggs into Catalina's basket. And Catalina is welcome to those eggs. Dealing with Grandma Victoria requires a computer brain. I would lose my patience and smush her.

Dina: Is that why you kept your grandfather's identity a secret after that incident in the hospital?

Arabella: Partly. Mostly I just liked having a bit of power

over the two of them. Let me tell you, you have never met two more manipulative people. When they met, it had to be fate, because they richly deserve each other. Keeping their hospital visit private gave me ammunition in case I needed to use it. When one of them started planning something nasty, I could wave it around and threaten to expose the whole thing. It worked better on Linus than Victoria.

I did have to excuse myself and laugh hysterically for a few minutes when it all came out. You should've seen Catalina's face. Ha! I shouldn't laugh, because she really went through hell with the two of them, but her expression! I wish I had snapped a pic.

Dina: So back to being nobody's favorite.

Arabella: Sure. We've covered grandparents. Mom is a person of great integrity. She tries so hard to keep everything equal, but if you watch her, you'll notice that she pays slightly more attention to Bern and Leon. They had an awful childhood until they came to live with us, and she's compensating a little. It's not that she loves me less. That's not it at all. It's that she focuses on Leon and Bern, and when they are okay, she usually ends up putting out fires with Nevada or Catalina. It's understandable. Nevada has baby Arthur, who might be a supervillain. I low-key keep waiting for him to accidentally destroy Houston because he can't find his sippy cup. Catalina deals with her Warden crap and tries to run the House. I...

Dina: Fall through the cracks?

Arabella: Sometimes. For example, when it was Bern's turn to go to college, we all had a lot of discussions about it. What major, how he was doing, how his grades were, and so on. Same with Nevada. When Catalina refused to go, it was a massive deal. Leon needed a lot of encouragement, and we all rooted for him. It was a group event to keep him on the path to graduation. I think we all should've gotten honorary degrees by the end of it, or like one of those coins military people get. Let me ask you, what's was my major?

Dina: Accounting?

Arabella: That's exactly what most of my family would say, except for Nevada, who saw my diploma. I double majored in Business Administration and Applied Magic Theory and got my degree in three years. I also have a Masters in Global Business and House Societies from Yale. I was admitted into the special semi-remote program for Primes there. To get in, you need a 3.8 GPA and two Prime sponsors who are not related to you. Really helps if one of them is an alumnus.

Dina: Who did you get?

Arabella: Augustine Montgomery and Stephen Jiang. I flew back and forth every other week for a year to attend debates and in-person lectures. I'd spend four days there and come back for ten. I paid for it out of my own pocket and told everyone I was going shopping up north. I would even bring back an outfit or two and parade around in them.

Dina: Did it work?

Arabella: Some. I knew when Leon figured it out because he started to make cute comments about my shopping trips. Leon is the best PI out of all of us. Alessandro tries very hard, but Leon is on another level. Maybe a tie with Nevada, except Nevada relies on truthseeking, and Leon is just that good. It's really hard to keep things from him. He's like a cat. Mom eventually told him to knock it off and stop hassling me, and that I lived in my own house and was allowed to have my own independence. I do love my little house on the edge of our lake. It's my sanctuary.

Dina: Does anyone else know?

Arabella: Bern. He needed me for something, and when I didn't answer my cell, he tracked my phone down to New

Haven and put two and two together. But I don't think Nevada knows. The grandparents and mom don't either, and Catalina for sure doesn't, because if she knew, she would've added my Masters degree to my agency bio. She's obsessive about it.

We're a family of PIs. Keeping a secret is pretty hard and I didn't exactly hide it that well. They don't know because they're not paying attention. That's what I mean by falling through the cracks.

Dina: How did they not figure out that you weren't keeping up with your regular workload?

Arabella: That's because I did keep up with it. Another thing I learned from Stephen is to maintain two separate workstations, each with their own workflow. I have two offices, one at my house and the other at our office pavilion. I color-coded everything. The two shall never meet.

Dina: Does this mean you've conquered math?

Arabella: Nope, still hate it. I hate it so, so much. I almost dropped out because I couldn't pass basic algebra. I dropped it three times and had to beg Bern for help. My poor cousin, heh. I think my math-stupidness broke his brain. Thank God for accounting software.

Dina: You've mentioned Stephen twice now. Are you two romantically involved?

Arabella: :laughs : No. Stephen is gēge, older brother. I help him with some… problems he encounters while doing business and we collaborate frequently. I did try to hit on him when we first met because I was young and naïve. I went through this phase where I crushed on various celebrities, and he was the first one I've met in person. Steven was very kind to me and made it clear that it would never happen. He also talked to me about taking risks. Some of the things I did back then would've made it easy for me to be taken advantage of. I've grown up a lot since then.

Dina: Will you tell us a bit about your magic?

Arabella: Of course not. There are two lovely people who created me, and I need to earn a living. If I give away all of my secrets, why would you buy my book?

Dina: Could you at least tell us what your plans are? Will you work for Baylor Investigative Agency forever?

Arabella: I'm not sure. It wasn't the original plan. At least I never saw myself doing it as a career. It was a great way to earn some money when I was a teenager, but when we became a House, it was all hands on deck. Most emerging Houses collapse within the first three years. The family needed me, so I did what I had to do. We are much more stable now. I'm not unhappy. Who knows, perhaps I will do something else in the future.

Dina: Thank you so much for spending time with us.

Arabella: Thank you for having me. I had a lovely time. And just so we are clear, I'm keeping these pastries. They're coming home with me.

AUGUSTINE MONTGOMERY

George: Mr. Montgomery, welcome. My name is George Camarine and I will be your interviewer today.

Augustine: It's a pleasure.

George: Coffee? Dessert?

Augustine: Yes, to both, thank you. The entremet looks delightful.

George: Doesn't it? Raspberry and white chocolate with a mascarpone mousse. The chef here is truly heavenly, and apparently a certain someone told him you are fond of these particular flavors.

Augustine: Ah, yes, the infamous Arabella interview. I'm surprised the Inn survived.

George: How did this mentor-mentee relationship come about?

Augustine: We had contracted a job out to the Baylor Investigative Agency, and they sent her to quibble about our referral fee. You might say I recognized a kindred soul. One could easily mistake her primary motivation as being purely financial, but it's deeper than that. She strives for personal excellence. Money is simply a tangible measure of winning. Being successful isn't enough. She wants to be so successful that she becomes a household name. Her sisters hide from fame, but Arabella seeks it out.

George: That can be a dangerous inclination.

Augustine: Very. Which was one of the reasons I took an interest. She needed guidance.

George: The situation with the Baylors is rather complicated, isn't it?

Augustine: An understatement.

George: Or perhaps an opening to a discussion.

Augustine: Very well. I met Nevada at a difficult point in my life. I had just fended off a particularly vicious attack on House Montgomery. My brother was taken. I had been stabbed several times. There was extensive blood loss, and it wasn't clear at the time if I would regain the full use of my left arm. It's not a particularly prudent thing for a man in my field to admit. I was at the end of my rope, and maintaining an illusion of perfect health and working limbs proved to be quite challenging.

I had to return to the office, to reassure our employees, to send a message to our enemies, and most importantly to coordinate the search for my sibling. We had to find Tarquin at all costs.

Instead, I'd arrived at my office that morning to be greeted by House Pierce having histrionics in my waiting room. Not taking the case wasn't an option. We owed Peter a favor, and he'd come to collect. In Prime society, a business runs on favors, and you are only as good as your ability to pay up. This is something that I had to impart onto Arabella. Raw power matters, but base matters more. Can you pick up the phone and call someone you haven't spoken to in two years, and compel them to do something that wouldn't be profitable for them, either to balance the books or to owe them a favor? Would they take that call? That's what being a Prime power means.

I was the only one among the MII personnel who could've

taken down Adam, and it would've been very difficult. I had to buy time, so I asked for the subcontractor with the best performance and got the Baylors. I gave them a cursory glance, because my time was in short supply, and they seemed to fit the bill. The plan was never to have them take down Pierce. I simply needed the appearance of an active investigation, and I counted on them being smart enough to keep from getting hurt.

Had I known Nevada would take this at face value, I would have… No, you know what, I would have done everything the same. In that particular state of mind, with what I knew at the time, I would've still made the same decision, because that's who I was back then.

George: But you are not that man now?

Augustine: My priorities have undergone a certain shift. The old adage says that if you beat a dog long enough, it will become vicious. I had been beaten for years in many ways. I had sunk very deep into the cycle of retaliation and pre-emptive measures. It took a catastrophic event to spark some self-awareness.

George: Connor threatening to kill you?

Augustine: That I had expected at the time. No, it was the fact that Nevada came to me. In her place, I would've eliminated me. It was cleaner and safer, while the alternative was messy and had questionable chances of success. She sat in my office, and I could tell that she was deeply conflicted. That woman genuinely didn't want to hurt me. It was another way to be. A way I strived for once, a long time ago, and had forgotten. As unbelievable as it seems, there was a time I was idealistic. Alas, House warfare doesn't suffer idealists.

George: Do you like yourself more now?

Augustine: I'd like to think so. I have drawn some lines, which I will not cross.

George: Did you recover your brother?

Augustine: Yes. He survived.

George: And your father's killer?

Augustine: smiling.

George: I see. Can you tell us a bit more about your family?

Augustine: I have two siblings and a cousin, whom I've taken in.

George: Are you romantically involved with anyone?

Augustine: Yes.

George: Is that all we're going to get? No details?

Augustine: Yes.

George: In that case, let's move on to a less sensitive subject. Konstantine Berezin.

Augustine: laughs.

George: Is he as good as he claims to be?

Augustine: Yes.

George: As good as you?

Augustine: No.

George: Why?

Augustine: Konstantine maintains his illusions sporadically during missions and in his spare time, for fun. I spent two years of my life pretending to be my dead father in front of high level illusion mages on our payroll. I've had significantly more practice, and my stakes were a lot higher.

George: Will we ever learn more about that?

Augustine: If they give me a book, you will. Without any false modesty, I believe I would be quite profitable for them.

George: False modesty serves no one.

Augustine: Indeed. So, tell me about yourself. What is it like to be married?

George: It is bliss. Let us conclude this interview, and I will tell you all about it.

Special preview avaliable on digital retailers!

Outlander meets *Game of Thrones* in this blockbuster new epic fantasy series from the #1 *New York Times* bestselling author duo Ilona Andrews.

When Maggie wakes up cold, filthy, and naked in a gutter, it doesn't take her long to recognize Kair Toren, a city she knows intimately from the pages of the famously unfinished dark fantasy series she's been obsessively reading and re-reading while waiting years for the final novel.

Her only tools for navigating this gritty world of rival warlords, magic, and mayhem? Her encyclopedic knowledge of the plot, the setting, and the characters' ambitions and fates. But while she quickly discovers she cannot be killed (though many will try!), the same cannot be said for the living, breathing characters she's coming to love—a motley band that includes a former lady's maid, a deadly assassin, various outrageous magical creatures, and a dangerously appealing soldier. Soon, instead of trying to get home, she finds herself enmeshed in the schemes—and attentions—of dueling princes, dukes, and villains, all while trying to save them and the kingdom of Rellas from the way she knows their stories will end: in a cataclysmic war.

For fans of Samantha Shannon, Danielle L. Jensen, Sarah J. Maas, and isekai and portal fantasy, This Kingdom Will Not Kill Me is the beginning of the most epic adventure yet from genre powerhouse author duo Ilona Andrews.

MAGIC BREAKS

MAGIC STEALS

MAGIC SHIFTS

MAGIC STARS

MAGIC BINDS

MAGIC TRIUMPHS

The Iron Covenant

IRON AND MAGIC

UNTITLED IRON AND MAGIC #2

Hidden Legacy Series

BURN FOR ME

WHITE HOT

WILDFIRE

DIAMOND FIRE

SAPPHIRE FLAMES

EMERALD BLAZE

RUBY FEVER

Innkeeper Chronicles Series

CLEAN SWEEP

SWEEP IN PEACE

ONE FELL SWEEP

SWEEP OF THE BLADE

SWEEP WITH ME

SWEEP OF THE HEART

Kinsmen

SILENT BLADE

SILVER SHARK

THE KINSMEN UNIVERSE (anthology with both SILENT BLADE
and SILVER SHARK)

FATED BLADES

The Edge Series

ON THE EDGE

BAYOU MOON

FATE'S EDGE

STEEL'S EDGE

ABOUT THE AUTHOR

Ilona Andrews is the pseudonym for a husband-and-wife writing team. Ilona is a native-born Russian and Gordon is a former communications sergeant in the U.S. Army. Contrary to popular belief, Gordon was never an intelligence officer with a license to kill, and Ilona was never the mysterious Russian spy who seduced him. They met in college, in English Composition 101, where Ilona got a better grade. (Gordon is still sore about that.)

Gordon and Ilona currently reside in Texas with their two children and many dogs and cats.

They have co-authored four *New York Times* and *USA Today* bestselling series, the urban fantasy of Kate Daniels, rustic fantasy of the Edge, paranormal romance of Hidden Legacy, and Innkeeper Chronicles, which they post as a free weekly serial. For complete list of their books, fun extras, and Innkeeper installments, please visit their website at www.ilona-andrews.com.